Dead Man's Trail

DEAD MAN'S TRAIL

by James Wesley

AVALON BOOKS

THOMAS BOUREGY AND COMPANY, INC.
22 EAST 60TH STREET • NEW YORK 10022

PRINTED IN THE UNITED STATES OF AMERICA
BY THE BOOK PRESS, BRATTLEBORO, VERMONT

Dead Man's Trail

CHAPTER ONE

Mark Nelson scowled as he sniffed the smelly main street of Nocariza. He had been in Mexican towns before, but none this small and dirty, none this far south of the border. It was an unhealthy place for gringos. Well, he hoped he wouldn't be here too long. Not that he was afraid.

For although Americans were looked upon with suspicion and often hatred, Mark felt safe in Nocariza. Sure, it was considered to be dangerous country. But he was under the protection of Jose Martinos, the governor of the province, from whom he intended to buy a passel of cheap Mexican cattle to augment his growing herd on the Culebra Range. He had come down here alone because he could find no trail hands willing to chance their lives in the

1

wild, desolate country, not even for bonus wages. The consensus of opinion was that nobody wanted to fight for a bonus he might not live to spend. But Mark knew that Red Teach was down here somewhere, and maybe Rex Nagle. They were both fugitives from justice in Arizona, but if either one or both of them would sign on as his *segundo*, he might keep the *vaqueros* Martinos had promised him, in line. Mark trusted Martinos, a handsome, angular man with curly black hair and dark eyebrows that formed a continuous line across his forehead. He trusted Martinos to furnish him with local cowhands sworn to loyalty. But even under the best circumstances, Latin temperaments could be a bit unpredictable.

Mark passed by some dreary-looking stores. Then, moments later, he paused before a doorless adobe *cantina* named *El Lobo*. The stench that issued from the place was anything but inviting. And it was noisy, too. There were sounds of coarse laughter, of arguments, and even the notes of a song that wafted through the babel with a sweet, sentimental refrain. It was a woman's voice, and Mark wondered what sort of woman would demean herself in such a questionable place.

He looked in through the door at the shadowy figures of men lined up at the bar. The only light in the room that reeked of tobacco and *cerveza* came through narrow slits in the adobe walls. As his eyes became accustomed to the dim light, he saw the girl with the guitar seated on one of the crude tables. It was difficult to make out her features, though he had the impression of a pale, angular face framed with dark hair.

Then his attention was drawn to one of the men at the bar. A shaft of light glinted off the tousled head of red hair. The man's sombrero hung down his back, Mexican style, and his stilted Spanish words and raucous laugh marked the man completely. He was Dave Teach, called Red on account of his hair. Mark took a deep breath and strode into the bedlam and stench. He walked up behind Teach and slapped him on the shoulder. Teach spun about and his gun appeared magically in his hand. His blue eyes glared at Mark until he recognized him. Then he let go a string of expletives both Mexican and American, with a few choice epithets of his own.

"You loco rannie. Don't you know better than to sneak up on a man when there's no mirror in the back bar to show you're comin'?" he demanded.

"Simmer down, Red. Ain't you glad to see me?" Mark grinned.

"This ain't no place for foolishment, Mark. You could be a dead man right this moment."

"If I was after you, Red, I would have stuck a knife in your back afore you could turn around. I been lookin' for you—you an' Rex Nagle."

"What the hell you doin' this far south of the border? You ain't no *bounty hunter* unless you've changed a lot." Red scowled.

"The bounty was canceled on you two years ago, Red. Oh, you're still wanted in Arizona, but there ain't no profit in bringin' you in dead or alive," Mark explained.

"Did you come all the way down here to tell me that?" Red inquired.

"No, Red. I come down here to buy cattle from Jose

Martinos. He claims to own most of the bush dogies, long horns, and what few white faces there are in the State of Sonora and part of Sinaloa."

"You goin' in fer raisin' scrubs?" Red demanded with veiled sarcasm.

Mark looked at the men lined up at the bar. The *cantina* was the one bright spot in their harsh lives. There were bandits here, *vaqueros*, and bar flies eking out a few centavos from skinning dead cattle, or from furs stripped from coyotes, badgers, or an occasional cougar, if they had the nerve and skill to bag one. They were men of primitive emotions, loud and noisy as they drank their tequila or mescal, but deadly and tenacious when crossed or insulted.

"Looky here, Red, I reckon I've already talked too much here," Mark said in a low voice. "These men ain't to be trusted. Do you reckon we can find a table in a corner where we won't be disturbed?"

Red nodded. Mark ordered two glasses and a bottle of tequila. The glasses were grimy but the potent liquor would kill any germ that came in contact with it. They found a table that was even darker than the rest of the room. An hombre with bristles sprouting from his swarthy face was dozing at the table with his head on his crossed arms. Red shook him awake, gave him a peso, and sent him to the bar to buy himself a drink. They were no sooner settled than the girl with the guitar came over and strummed lightly on the strings. She settled herself near Mark.

"You are new here, senor. What you do, a man like you, among the pigs of thees *pueblo* of Nocariza? I hear the rumor, senor, you weesh to drive a herd of these runty cattle up north to the river. This a bad way, senor. The *vaqueros* call eet *Pista del Muerto*, the trail of death."

"Lolita," Teach admonished her, "what did I tell you about pickin' up strangers? You're my girl, remember?"

"I am nobody's girl, Senor Teach. You teach me the *Ingles*. You buy for me the guitar and tell me to sing in the *cantina*, but you no buy me with these theengs. I tell you about the *Pista del Muerto*. Perhaps you mean to rob this hombre yourself!" she snapped.

"Senor Nelson is my *amigo*, Lolita. You get out of here before I paddle your bottom!" Red admonished her.

Lolita left, swinging her hips provocatively.

"She's a purty wench," Mark told him. "Why don't you marry her?"

"Because I'll never be ready to settle down," Red said. "Now let's hear more of your get-rich-quick scheme, Mark."

"It ain't a matter of gettin' rich quick. It's a matter of gettin' rich slow but solid. I've got good graze on the Culebra Range, and enough water. Cattle up north sell for twenty to forty dollars a head. Here I can get 'em for two dollars a head, with the bulls thrown in."

"Some bulls. They got the pedigree of a skunk," Red ribbed him.

"They'll do. I aim to get some thoroughbred bulls later. On my range these runty cattle will get fat an' the bulls will get strong," Mark averred.

"What Lolita told you about the trail from here to Rio Grande ain't far from wrong. The *bandidos* might let you alone because they fear Jose Martinos, but the Indians down this way won't give a damn. Then there's the wolves an' the coyotes to be reckoned with. Why don't you go back an' rustle your way to riches? That's the way the big ranches got started."

"I said I aim to grow slow, but solid. How long do you think I'd last stealin' cattle? This ain't the olden days. Right after the war, the bush was full of cattle that had strayed with no one to ride herd on 'em. The first trail drives were made up of hides an' bones that took a lot of eastern corn to fatten them up fit to eat."

Red shrugged. "I reckon you might starve before the cattle do. What's your proposition an' where do I fit in?"

"Martinos has promised to furnish me with *vaqueros* which he claims are loyal to him," Mark explained.

"Mebbe too loyal," Red hinted.

"What do you mean?" Mark asked.

"Martinos has got your money, ain't he?"

"I reckon that's the way things is done," Mark said. "You pay your money and you get the goods."

"You're gettin' two, mebbe three or four thousand head of critters with four legs an' lousy dispositions. Did it ever occur to you that Martinos might give his men instructions to kill you, take back the cattle, and blame it all on *bandidos* or Indians?"

"Hold it, Red! They's gotta be some trust in the world. Martinos has a reputation for shootin' square. Why would he want to take my herd back? He's got more cattle than he can count runnin' loose here in Sonora and Sinaloa provinces."

"There ain't no rich hombre who don't crave more riches. There's a rumor that anybody caught stealin'

Martinos cattle is shot without benefit of law. If he don't give the *vaqueros* orders to take over the herd, they might get a notion to drive the herd to the river, an' then take over before the critters get their feet wet."

"That brings up the point of why I searched you out, Red. I heard you was down thisaway an' Nocariza is the most likely *pueblo* south of Agua Prieta. I was hopin' to find Rex Nagle with you. The three of us should be a match for the *vaqueros* if they try anything funny."

"Rex got wind of a bounty hunter on his trail. He headed for Ocompo, which is a *bandido* hangout. The posters are still out on him. He killed the wrong man by mistake. He never could control his temper," Teach said.

"Do you think you could wheedle him out of Ocompo? It ain't a far piece south of here."

"Why do you think he might side with you, Mark? You an' me is friends from a far piece back, but Rex scarcely knowed you."

"He can name his own price, Red. He don't have to cross the border, just help get the cattle to the Rio Grande."

"How many *vaqueros* is Martinos sendin' along?"

"About a dozen."

"I reckon we could handle them—mebbe—if they don't have an ambush arranged halfway to the States. That is, *if* I can persuade Nagle to come along."

"Give it a try, Red. Let's get outta here, I'm suffocatin'," Mark said.

They rose from their stools and headed for the open doorway. When they reached the crowded center of the *cantina*, a big, brazen brute of a man was manhandling

Lolita. He held her in his hairy paws and laughed loudly at her discomfiture.

Lolita was crying. "You're hurting me, you pig!" she screamed.

Her scream only intensified the brute's attack. He tried to force a kiss on her and ripped away the front of her dress. Mark barged in, acting instinctively. That he was on alien ground made no difference to the explosive thrust of his emotions. He twisted the brute's arm until he let the girl go. Then he threw a punch at the big man's greasy face. The other men in the smelly room backed up against the bar and the adobe walls. The big man roared in surprise at this sudden attack. Before he could gather his wits, Mark sent another blow to his stomach which doubled him up. Gasping and weaving to get his balance, the brute exploded.

"*Madre de Dios!* You loco gringo! I, Luis Velasco, shall keel you for this thing you do me!"

Mark realized he was in for a fight, but there was no turning back. That Lolita had warned him of the dangers on the *Pista del Muerto* made her his *amiga*, more or less. Besides, he could never stand by and see a woman mauled and degraded by a brutish man. He braced himself waiting for Velasco to go for his gun. Then he realized that Velasco had no sidearm. Velasco came at him, his hairy fists flailing, his long arms reaching to grasp Mark in a bear hug. Mark dodged the apelike arms and his sombrero went skittering across the littered floor. He straightened up and threw a punch at the side of Velasco's hairy face. The big man, bewildered by the gringo who danced out of reach of his big fists, let out a roar and turned. Head lowered, he charged Mark like an angry bull. His sombrero was being trampled underfoot and his stringy black hair hung over his bleary eyes. Mark caught the charge on his hip and the sheer weight of it spun him to the earthen floor. Velasco loomed over him, lifting his booted foot to drive his star-roweled spur into Mark's face. Mark caught the foot as it descended and with a mighty effort twisted it until Velasco fell in a snarling heap to one side.

—Mark staggered to his feet. He stared at the circle of brown faces contorted with a lust for blood or worse. He couldn't see Red Teach in the crowd. That suited him. It was his fight and he had to finish it win, lose, or draw. He waited for his opponent to get halfway to his feet. Then he leaped in and rammed a boot heel into Velasco's paunchy stomach. Velasco doubled up and air whooshed from his lungs. He fell over backward and lay gasping for air. Mark, himself unsteady, reached for his hat and his gun, which had slid from the holster. As he straightened up, he heard a cry behind him. It was Teach's voice.

"Look out, he's got a knife!"

Mark whirled just as the knife flashed down. He felt the blade briefly pierce the flesh of his shoulder. He still had his gun in his hand. He brought it down on Luis Velasco's bare head with all the force he could muster. The big man fell like a pole-axed ox.

"*Ole!*" some of the men shouted, proving that Velasco had enemies in the crowd.

Red Teach reached his side as Mark headed for the doorway. "Let's get out of here before Velasco comes to his senses. These men cheered a gringo who has just beaten their champ to the floor. That would be an insult that Velasco could not take lying down."

They found Lolita waiting outside the doorway. She had managed to pull her torn dress together. She looked up at Mark, her dark eyes soft with sympathy.

"Senor, you lose the blood!" she exclaimed. "For me you fight like the matador fight the bull!"

"Not just for you, honey," Mark mumbled, trying to staunch the blood with his hand, "but for all women against bullies."

"I must take care for you. You come to my house. My *madre*, she fix you up pronto," Lolita insisted.

"Better go with her, Mark. There ain't no medico in this town fit to doctor a dog," Teach suggested.

Mark followed the girl, who had a firm grip on his belt. They stumbled through the littered streets, avoiding the worst chuckholes. They passed some squalid adobe hovels from which people watched them pass. Then Lolita urged him into one of the adobes. Weakened by the loss of blood, he submitted to her.

Inside was an open corridor with no roof that admitted the sunlight. The earthen floor was hard as stone and swept clean. On either side of the passage he saw neat, orderly beds covered with patchwork quilts. Bleached sheepskins lay before the beds. Then they arrived in the larger room in which was a fireplace and chairs made of mesquite and woven willow reeds or leather thongs. A rotund woman with a moon face stared at them without surprise but with a frown of resignation.

"What you bring here now, Lolita? Another of your stupid *amigos* in need of fixing up?" she said.

"This is no one of my *amigos, madre.* He is gringo who fight for me. He is lose the blood."

"Always some stupid hombre fight for you, *muchacha,*" the mother said. She gave Mark a closer look and saw the blood dripping from his shirt. "Sit down, hombre. Get me some tequila, Lolita," she ordered as she unbuttoned Mark's shirt.

"Let me help you, senora," Teach offered. He slipped the bloody shirt off Mark's shoulders. Blood was trickling from the knife wound.

"This is bad cut," the woman said, shaking her head. "But it could be more bad. I will fix up."

Lolita came with the tequila and the older woman poured some in the wound. Mark winced at the burn of the alcohol and let out a gasp.

"It no keel you," the woman said. "If you fight the bull, you get the horn. What you do here in Nocariza?"

"I came to see Jose Martinos," Mark told her.

The woman said something in Spanish to Lolita. Lolita went to a box in one corner of the room and came back with some clean cloths and a fresh shirt. Her mother staunched the blood from the knife wound and proceeded to make a pad to cover the wound. She smeared the pad with a foul-smelling concoction which Lolita brought her and, drawing the edges of the cut together, she covered it with the pad. As she bound the pad in place, she talked.

"What's your name?" she asked in Spanish.

Mark was conversant with Spanish; one had to be so close to the border. "My name is Mark Nelson," he told her. "What is your name?"

There was a brief pause.

"My name is Maria. You are a friend of Jose Martinos?"

"Yes, senora."

"You don't have his protection?"

"This ruckus was my fault, Maria."

"Who cut you up?" Maria asked him.

Lolita answered for him. "Luis Velasco cut him up. Luis try to get fresh with me. He tear my dress off me," she said accusingly.

"Luis is a good man if he leaves alone the mescal. You're lucky he didn't kill you, Senor Nelson. Where is Luis now?" Maria asked.

"Last I saw of him, he was layin' on the floor of the *cantina* out cold," Mark told her.

"You kill him?"

"No, I didn't kill him. I knocked him out with my gun before he could get a second slice of me," Mark told her.

"You make a bad enemy, senor. Better you had killed him. He will kill you one day. Here, put on this shirt. It is clean."

"I ain't a killer, senora," he said. He put on the shirt.

"It's better you leave Nocariza, Senor Mark Nelson."

"Not until I've completed my business. Here, take this for your trouble, Maria." He offered her five pesos.

She refused the money. "Jose Martinos take care of his *amigos*. Once I saved his life. I weel never starve."

Mark didn't argue the point, knowing it would be useless. "I'm going to Martinos's *hacienda*, Maria. I will tell him what you did for me. He will make it up to you."

Outside the house, Mark said to Teach, "You go find Rex Nagle, Red. I got a notion we'll need him. I'm riding out to see Jose. He should have the herd gathered in the next few days."

As Teach left, Lolita came out of the house. "You are weak like the kitten, senor, from losing the blood. You need a nurse. Besides, Jose Martinos ees my godfather. I go to the *hacienda* with you."

CHAPTER TWO

Don Jose Martinos's *Casa Grande*, the big house, was surrounded by adobe walls two feet thick to repel the invasion of wild boars or stray bulls. They were whitewashed to the purity of new snow. Outside the walls, the short flush of spring flowers was in full bloom. Red cactus roses stared defiantly from their thorny stalks, and golden poppies with their red throats grew in profuse clusters among the gentle blue lupine.

Inside the walls the gardens were a riot of disciplined beauty. A tributary of the Rio Yaqui, fed by live springs, watered the area and provided water for the fountain that trickled over the rocks in the center of a flowerbed.

Seated in the patio with Don Jose, Mark Nelson fingered his delicate glass, half-filled with brandy

14

imported from Spain, and studied Martinos. His handsome face—with its aristocratic nose, its black eyebrows that formed a continuous line across his eyes, and its shock of dark, wavy hair—was a disarming facade for the deeper character of the man behind it. Don Jose had complete authority in this isolated corner of Mexico. Mark came straight to the point.

"I ain't got much time to hang around Nocariza and quibble, Don Jose. I reckon I've stirred up some trouble that could get worse if I hang around here."

Don Jose puffed softly on his cigar. "There is no trouble in the province that I cannot mediate, Senor Nelson," he said meditatively.

Mark opened his shirt and exposed the bandage on his shoulder. "Can you mediate that, Don Jose?" Mark said grimly.

"Certainly," the don said without changing his expression. "I shall have the man shot."

Mark winced, taking Don Jose at his word. "I reckon that's a mite drastic, ain't it? It was partly my fault."

"Would you explain that, senor?"

"A bully was manhandling a girl—the one who came here with me. He tore her dress half off her. I couldn't stand still for it. I dragged him away from her and we got into a fight. He took a knife to me when my back was turned."

"Did you kill him?"

"No, I knocked him out with my gun."

"Who was this despoiler of women?"

"I was told his name is Luis Velasco," Mark replied.

Don Jose appeared to stiffen at the mention of the

name. "Yes, *amigo*, you are in trouble. While you are here you are under my protection, but out on the trail—"

Mark cut him off. "What d'you mean, out on the trail?"

"Luis Velasco is my *primero* trail drover. He has his own crew of men. Trusting a herd to Velasco is a guarantee of safe delivery. His crew will get you safely to the Rio Grande. He understands the Indians, and *bandidos* are careful not to incur his wrath."

"Hold everything, Don Jose!" Mark exclaimed. "I got about as much chance of survivin' in his company as I would have finding a cool place in hell."

"He will honor my orders to get your herd safely to the border. After that you will have to settle with him."

"The prospect ain't very rosy, Don Jose," Mark objected.

"Without him there would be no roses at all, senor, except perhaps a cactus rose or two pushing up among your bones. Besides, I have another reason for sending him."

"It had better be a good one," Mark warned.

"Porfirio Diaz, the president, is sending a detachment of cavalry to check on the province and collect the yearly tax. There could be some trouble. I must remain here, but I wish to send my wife and daughter to the United States with you. My daughter is to go to the San Xavier Mission near Elfrida."

It took a moment for this to sink in. Mark had never met Don Jose's wife or daughter, who mostly kept to the seclusion of their quarters. He envisioned a brat without manners, spoiled by an indulgent father, and a fleshy Spanish woman gone to seed because of the isolation. As though on cue from an invisible stage director, Lolita and a Spanish senorita, slim and beautiful, invaded the patio.

Don Jose rose and frowned his displeasure. "Have I sent for you, Magdalena?" he said firmly.

"No, Father, but Lolita told me about the young man who saved her from disgrace. I had to meet him," Magdalena said, smiling. Her skin was like cream, without a blemish. Her eyes under her crown of dark hair glowed with excitement. "I am Magdalena, the despair of my father's life," she said to Mark before her father could speak.

"Why did your mother allow this?" Don Jose demanded.

The answer came from another quarter. A lady appeared from the house, her green satin dress reflecting the sunlight. She wore a silk shawl about her slim shoulders, and a mantilla hung down over the jeweled comb that held her neat chignon.

"I have allowed it, Jose," the woman said in perfect English, "because if we are traveling under the protection of Senor Nelson, we should at least meet with our host."

"Pardon me, ma'am," Mark interrupted her. "I reckon we're both subject to another host."

"And who can that be?" Senora Martinos asked.

"I've been told his name is Luis Velasco," Mark replied.

"That gorilla?" The senora's black eyebrows raised, and she pursed her carmine lips. It was evident she had made up her face before emerging from the house.

"Call him what you like, Estrella. If he is a *gorilla*, he is a trained gorilla, honest to me, and loyal. Through the country you are traversing, you could not be in better hands," Don Jose said.

Lolita spoke up. "I was in his hands, Senora Martinos.

They are strong hands. He try to tear my clothes off. Also he ees cunning. He try to knife Senor Mark in the back."

"*Muchacha*," Don Jose said, "I don't know why Magdalena insists on befriending you."

"Because she is the only girl in Nocariza near my age who speaks English," Magdalena said. "What she just said is the truth."

"Am I to be disputed by the women of my *hacienda*? When a man has spent weeks on the range gathering wild cattle, he sometimes drinks too much when he goes to a bar. Luis is a man and Lolita is a girl. If she wishes to be treated like an innocent, she should be in a convent. You are my wife and daughter. He will treat you accordingly. He will keep you safe until you reach Arizona. There will be no liquor on the trail drive. Luis knows my rules and lives by them. The cattle have been gathered. The wagons have been provisioned. You will start in three days."

"Just a minute, senor," Mark said. "Ain't it customary to have a count of the cattle and some sort of a road brand?"

"A waste of time, Senor Nelson. You will find more cattle in the herd than you bargained for. The less cattle the tax collector finds, the less taxes I will pay. Diaz needs money for his social reforms. From me he would demand more than the cattle are worth. I will give you a bill of sale. It will be honored."

Three days later, Mark found himself on the trail. Dave Teach had brought Rex Nagle along with him. Rex was a big man, well proportioned. He had a knife scar across his strong jaw, and his coarse black hair was raked across a bullet groove in his scalp. There was no truculence about him, but there was a subdued threat of menace that was more effective than harsh words. He wore his guns lower than most and no one disputed the notches in their ivory butts. Mark found himself, along with Dave and Rex, isolated from the dozen *vaqueros* and horse wranglers who took orders from no one but Velasco. They ate the same food as the *vaqueros* but the camaraderie ended there. Mark recalled Red's warning that Martinos might have his *vaqueros* take the cattle back and blame the raid on Indians or bandits. To Mark's surprise, Red Teach brought the subject up again. They were seated in the circle of light created by a small fire of cow dung and mesquite stalks.

"This is a big, empty country, Mark. It's fit only for iguanas, rattlesnakes, an' gophers. They live by eatin' one another. We're three trustin' gringos agin a dozen Mex who are loyal to only one man. Like I said before, they could cut our throats in our sleep, make off with the herd, an' blame it on the Yaqui or *bandidos*."

"Wait a minute, Red. We got insurance," Mark reminded him.

"What kind of insurance?"

"The women in that fancy wagon close to our camp. There's the Senora Martinos, Lolita who Magdalena insisted come along as her companion, Magdalena's duenna, and the old man who's drivin' their wagon. If Luis, or his *vaqueros*, killed us they would have to kill the whole shebang. If Don Jose learned of their crime, he would have them all shot. If anything happens to us or the women, he'd kill them anyway for letting it happen."

For long days they drove the cattle north. Luis Velasco had apologized to Mark for causing the trouble in the canteen, blaming it on the mescal, but as *jefe* of the trail, he insisted that Mark and his two cowboys take their turn at riding drag, the dustiest, most troublesome position on the drive. The wild cattle were constantly breaking out of the herd, and it was the drag riders who had to force them back in.

The special trail wagon in which the women traveled, with Magdalena's duenna as cook and housekeeper, moved a little in advance of the herd to avoid the smell and the dust. The girls had horses of their own, tied to their wagon, and they rode them at times, racing across the high plateau. They were an odd pair, a girl from the alley of the *pueblo*, and the princess of the *hacienda*. One day when he was riding point, Mark was surprised to find Magdalena riding beside him.

"What's the matter, Mark? We women aren't contaminated. You could stop by and say hello now and then. How about supper tonight?" she dared him.

"Look, senorita—"

"Don't call me senorita," she interrupted him, "call me Magdalena."

"Are you tryin' to cause trouble, Magdalena? You ain't supposed to be here near the *vaqueros*."

"They wouldn't dare touch me," she said confidently.

"Don't be too sure about that. Your father pays them and Luis keeps them in line, but they're half primitive men. Your father's pesos might buy their obedience, but not their hearts. Remember, you're a beautiful woman, and above everything men want beautiful women."

"I'm prepared to take care of myself, Mark." She covertly showed him the small, but deadly, gun in the pocket of her divided skirt.

"A gun is as deadly as the person behind it, Magdalena. You couldn't kill a man."

"My mother did, once. He was no peon, either," she retorted.

"Go back to your wagon, and save me the worry of further trouble," Mark advised her.

"Are you afraid of trouble, Mark? Isn't that what life's all about—trouble? Is that why you're single, Mark? Would a wife be too much trouble?"

"There ain't no use for us to discuss that. You ain't cut out to be the wife of a down-at-the-heels cowboy."

"Why? Because my father is the governor of a province? That doesn't make me less of a woman, Mark. A woman has a heart and a mind and emotions in spite of her position in life. I'm attracted to you. You're a man with purpose and courage. Your fight in the *cantina* proved you are willing to take a beating to protect the honor of any person, no matter what their station in life."

"When the nuns at the convent get through with you, Magdalena, you'll see things in a different light. You'll see we come from two different worlds."

The arrival of Luis Velasco ended their discussion. Shaved and couth without the reek of liquor about him, he was an impressive figure. His strong face, with its deep-set eyes, reflected the image of a man who understood his authority and meant to exercise it.

"Senorita Martinos, it would be more better eef you avoid the dust and smell of the cattle," he suggested softly.

"Why don't you mind your own business, Luis?" she chastised him.

"You are my business, senorita. Stay where you belong and nothing will happen to you. *Comprende?*"

"You'd better go, Magdalena. Luis is right, this is no place for you," Mark said.

"You are the owner of this herd, Mark. You don't have to take orders from your trail boss." With that she rode away.

That night over their beans and meat, washed down with generous cups of Mexican coffee, Mark talked with Teach and Nagle. They sat apart from the *vaqueros*, one of whom was strumming a guitar and singing a soft love song.

"Mark," Teach said, his red hair reflecting the light of the small fire they had built, "are you plumb sure Velasco is headin' us in the right direction?"

"What do you mean?" Mark asked, puzzled.

"He could be anglin' toward the east. That would take us close to Chihuahua an' end us up in El Paso. There we would have to cross the Rio Grande and it could be at flood stage this time of year. If we headed directly north, we'd come out between Bisbee and Nogales an' we wouldn't have to cross the Rio."

"So you still think he's goin' to take the herd over an' kill the lot of us, is that it?" Mark grinned.

"I ain't never had much trust in a greaser," Red mumbled.

"There's all kinds of greasers, just like there's all kinds of gringos," Mark said.

"Granted, but the Mex are revolution minded. They

hate authority. Even Diaz with all his reforms can't please them. He's spending most of the money around Mexico City, and the northern provinces feel neglected. I ain't sure they got much love for Don Jose or his family. They fear him because he holds their lives in his hands, but they're loyal to Luis Velasco because he turns his head if they want to do a little stealing on the side."

"Forget it. They can't steal the herd without gettin' rid of us. If they get rid of us, they'll have to get rid of the women. They'd never get away with that an' they know it," Mark reassured them.

"I ain't so sure of that," Nagle said, siding with Red.

"Why? What's on your mind, Rex?" Mark asked.

"If they're goin' to blame it on Indians, they could go whole hog. Indians have staged more'n one massacre, leavin' nobody alive. The cattle herd would be enough incentive."

Mark mulled this over. There was an element of truth in their allegations. Massacres had been staged by white men, too. Senseless massacres for revenge or greed. But massacres were things of the past. Even the backward Indians of Mexico must have learned that a brutal attack on this trail drive could bring about reprisals that could eliminate them completely. Besides, Velasco would have an insurmountable task if he tried to sell off the herd even at cut-rate prices.

"You all are thinkin' poppycock an' you know it," Mark told them.

"Mebbe you're right," Red agreed.

Two days later they found good graze along the Yaqui River. Mark suggested that they stay over for a couple of days in the *pueblo* of Santa Barbara, which had grown up along the road from the silver mine in the hills nearby. Luis agreed somewhat reluctantly. The river made a loop here creating a sizable pool of water, which should keep the cattle from straying.

"We can put out some salt blocks to keep the cattle quiet and, besides, the men deserve a break," Mark argued.

"Senor Nelson, the men will break one another's necks once they get the taste of tequila and mescal. That's the kind of break they will get. You see what happen to me in Nocariza—go loco. I cut you up."

"Forget it, Luis. I've seen drunks killed over the drop of a word, but it never stopped anybody from drinkin'. The cut you gave me is healed."

"How about the women, senor? The *alcaldes*—the mayors—of these isolated *pueblos* resent the authority of Don Jose. They could resent the presence of Don Jose's women."

"Leave the women to me, Luis. They deserve a rest from the wagon and a chance to clean themselves properly," Mark assured him.

"Eef you are a man of honor, senor, why do you not have a woman of your own?" Luis demanded.

"I have a woman, Luis," Mark said.

"Why you come away from her?"

"Her name is Delma Ford. Her father owns a big ranch next to mine."

"Her father, he approve for you to have this woman?"

"On one condition, Luis."

"What condition must you fulfill to possess this Delma Ford?"

"I must prove that I can build up a herd of my own. That's one of the reasons I came to Mexico to buy cheap cattle. If you got any fears about my conduct with Magdalena, forget them. She's lonely and has been cooped up most of her life. I'm sure her mother will see she ain't harmed."

Suddenly the subject changed to love.

"Any man should experience love once in his life—I have," Velasco said.

"What happened, Luis?"

"She was killed by an assassin's bullet."

"Oh?" Mark whispered the word. He thought of Delma, his own love. Delma had no delusions of grandeur, nor did Dale Ford, her father. Delma was a western girl, loving the land she lived in, but she was no moon-eyed filly. She was four years younger than Mark, but she knew the rigors and the demands of the West. She didn't try to flout her father's conditions but accepted them with one or two minor objections.

"Pa's afraid some city slicker with a smooth tongue and foxy brain will woo me for the sake of getting the ranch after he's dead. He also figures I'm worth more than a roving cowboy. That's why he wants you to prove yourself, Mark," she had told him. "But why go to Mexico for cattle? You can get cattle here. Mexico is a dangerous land for gringos. There are hombres down there who would slit your throat for a peso."

"I'll miss you, Delma," he had explained to her the last

time he saw her in Douglas. "But you're smart enough to know that I can get many more cattle down there for my money than I can get here."

It was tough leaving her. She had cried when he left, and she had resented her tears. She was not the crying type. The sight of her puddled eyes when he had kissed her good-bye stayed with him until now. Her unguarded emotion had almost forced him to abandon his plan. He had reluctantly offered to do so, but she objected.

"No, Mark, that wouldn't work. You would always remember that it was my tears that persuaded you to change your plans. I wouldn't respect you for giving in to me. I wouldn't respect myself for asking you to. A woman who gets her way through tears is no more than a petulant child. Go for your Mexican cattle with my blessing, and come back real quick."

They would be back in Arizona in a few weeks if everything went smoothly.

"Luis, you go ahead and give your men the word. One man must stay with the herd at all times while the others are in town. I'll tell the women about our plans."

Luis gave him a long look, but he made no objections. He turned and rode toward the herd to give his *vaqueros* instructions. Mark rode to where the fancy wagon carrying the women had stopped. The old driver met him outside the wagon.

"What's the matter, senor?" the old man asked.

"Nothing is wrong, old man," Mark assured him. "I must talk with the Senora Martinos."

The driver went inside the wagon and came out with the duenna.

"What you want, senor?" the buxom woman asked.

"We are going to stop in this *pueblo* for a couple of days to rest up the herd and ourselves."

Magdalena's head popped out of the door. "You mean we're going to have a real bath and clean clothes? I love you, Mark Nelson," she bantered. "I've loved you since I first set eyes on you!"

CHAPTER THREE

The *pueblo* of Santa Barbara was a collection of adobe buildings built along a littered dusty street. There were a few shops with meager wares—a shoe store, a bakery, a trading post that bartered with the Indians for their crude but artistic silver crucifixes and images of the saints. The *alcalde's* residence stood apart, near the center of the town. It was a large house surrounded by a wall of loose rocks, its colorful gardens watered by a live spring that miraculously gushed from a nearby ledge of rock. The invading Spaniards had subdued the natives with cannon and blunderbusses, while the accompanying *padres* had saved their souls with gentle persuasion. The inevitable church at the end of the crooked street blocked the way, as though to compel attention. It was built of adobe, like

They go back to the *cantina* to get the medicine that make them sick in the first place."

Mark rode just ahead of the women's wagon, his keen eyes probing every unglazed window and open door. Some of these outlying towns were havens for bandits, murderers, and vagabonds. Teach and Nagle rode behind the wagon to prevent trouble. The *vaqueros*, eager for the taste of tequila, raced ahead into the town shooting off their revolvers. There was no way to tone down their exuberance outside of pure force, which would only add to the confusion. The townspeople, waking up from their afternoon siestas, came out of their mud-thatched adobes to stare at them, some in fear and some with welcome. The young girls waved at them and threw them kisses until their mothers slapped their arms down. Luis Velasco came up to ride beside Mark.

"Do you think your men will cause trouble, Luis?" Mark asked.

"Who knows, senor? A man's spirit can be contained just so long. These *vaqueros* have had the long, dusty ride. For tonight they wash the memory of eet away in tequila, and perhaps the kiss of a senorita. I have been there myself, senor, I understand."

Yes, Velasco had been there himself in Nocariza. Mark could still feel the twitch in the scar of his knife wound.

"Our women must be protected, Luis," Mark warned him.

"*Si, si*, senor. We will make first a visit to the *alcalde*. He will give them his protection."

"Are there bandits holed up here?" Mark asked.

"Who knows? The silver mines give some of the peons

work. This ees not enough. Don Pietro Oliviera accepts
tribute as a means for survival. He asks no man the source
of his income. To him money has no smell. In the *pueblo*
you are safe as een the house of God. Outside, you are on
your own."

They left the main road and took a half-circle drive that
brought them to the gate of the garden. Magdalena was
scrambling out of the wagon before Mark could dismount
and get around to help her. It was Rex Nagle who caught
her in his arms as she jumped from the high step of the
wagon. Her mother climbed down more sedately, aware
of her position. As the senora gave Mark her hand to help
her from the high step, she said in an undertone:

"I'm not sure we'll be as safe here as we would be in the
cantina. Don Pietro Oliviera and my husband seldom
agreed on anything. I'll see if I can wangle you quarters in
the house. Senors Teach and Nagle will no doubt prefer
the *cantina*. There will be little conviviality here."

"Mebbe I'd better join the other peons?" Mark
suggested.

She squeezed his arm. "As a favor to me, stay in the
house. I'll need moral support."

Velasco instructed the old driver to take the horses and
wagon to the barn in the rear of the house, and have the
horses cared for and the wagon scrubbed and cleaned
inside and out.

"I reckon there won't be time to do all that," Mark
objected, overhearing the instructions.

"Senor Nelson, thees is *manana* land. Tonight the
vaqueros stay up drinking all night. Tomorrow they sleep
all day. They wake up feeling—how you say?—lousy.

go back to the *cantina* to get the medicine that make them sick in the first place."

Mark frowned. "How long will we be hung up here?"

"Three, perhaps four days. Who knows?"

That prediction sobered Mark. He had expected to be across the border within two weeks if they made good progress. Perhaps this stopover was a mistake. Delma would be waiting for him and any long delay might worry her. He missed the feel of her lips on his. He missed her smile, her laughter. He shrugged. The cattle business wasn't run by a clock or a calendar. He knew few cowboys who had either of them. Luis offered to introduce them to the *alcalde*. Senora Martinos refused the offer.

"I'll introduce myself to the old goat. I don't expect a royal welcome."

Luis was glad to escape and join his men. As the senora had predicted, Red and Rex were eager to join Luis. Magdalena took hold of Mark's arm. "You will be my bravo *caballero*, Mark. If Don Pietro has daughters, I want them to envy me."

The duenna bustled forward and removed Magdalena's hand from Mark's arm.

"I'm not a girl anymore, Elena. I am a woman, and I'm not being too familiar with Mark Nelson," Magdalena snapped, replacing her hand.

Lolita, who had tarried in the wagon to redden her lips and darken her already dark eyebrows, took a place at Mark's other side.

"Now you will have two senoritas, Senor Mark," she said with a toss of her head.

"You look like a flirt, Lolita." Elena frowned.

"Perhaps Don Pietro will like a little flirting," Lolita responded.

"I doubt Don Pietro will enjoy a flirtation, not if I have remembered his wife, Rosita," the senora said. "She was no beauty the last time I saw her in Nocariza. She must be fat and ugly by now, but she is insanely jealous. Pull the bell rope, Elena."

They crossed the wide veranda of the impressive residence of the *alcalde*. A bell clanged somewhere inside the house and presently the door was opened by an elderly servant in a faded silk tunic, decorated with white braid, and pantaloons too tight for his bulging body. It was evident that Don Pietro or his wife, Rosita, still clung to the elegance of Spain.

"I am Dona Estrella Martinos, wife of Don Jose Martinos. I seek shelter for me and my party. Please inform Don Pietro Oliviera," Senora Martinos said.

The old man stood for a moment, his eyes bulging in wonder. It was evident they had few visitors of status here in the *pueblo*.

"Go, pronto!" the senora said impatiently.

"*Si, si*, senora," the man squeaked and vanished.

Soon there appeared an imposing figure with an adequate paunch which was adorned by a red sash. He spread his short arms at sight of them.

"*Madre di Dios!*" he exclaimed. "What misfortune has led you to this godforsaken country, senora? Has the revolution broken out again?"

"No, Don Pietro, Porfirio Diaz is still in control. I'll explain it to you after we have rested, cleaned ourselves, and had a glass of wine. May we come in?"

He stood back and made a sweeping motion with one arm. "Of course, senora. We are honored by your visit."

They entered the cool, inviting rooms, dimly lit by slit windows reminiscent of a fortress. The furniture was old but beautiful. There was a curved stairway in the entry that led to the upstairs rooms. To their left they entered a room with a tiled floor that was covered at random with Indian rugs. There was a beautiful table with curved legs, which was flanked by two upholstered chairs covered with needlepoint displaying a colorful design of leaves. From there they entered a room with more primitive furniture, but it was equally impressive. There was an air of emptiness about the house.

"Are you living here alone, Senor Oliviera?" Senora Martinos asked. "I trust nothing has happened to your family."

"My sons and my daughter are in Mexico City at the university. I doubt they will ever return to Santa Barbara." Don Pietro shrugged.

"I wouldn't blame them. It seems that Saint Barbara is neglecting her namesake."

"Not entirely, senora. She has provided the silver that sustains us," he reminded her.

"And the Dona Rosita, is she still well?" Senora Martinos asked.

"She is well physically, but in the mind she is still a shrew. She blames me for this isolation. Now she is worried about the weather, as though I can do something about it. She resents the fact that the children have grown up and left home. I would be better off with a half-breed Yaqui wife, but the church forbids divorce."

"Come, come, Don Pietro, it can't be that bad. Nocariza is no metropolis, but we manage to survive there," the senora chided him.

Before he could reply, they emerged from the corridor into an enclosed patio, its roof open to the sky. It was a pleasant garden with the mingled scents of many flowers, and the walls were covered with Indian art. Dona Rosita was draped on a chaise longue and Dona Estrella was surprised at her appearance. She was not fat and ugly. She was no outstanding beauty, but she had a certain charm. She had kept her shape well, considering the diet in this isolated place. At the sight of Estrella, the girls, and Mark Nelson, she rose with regal grace and her face lit up. She threw her arms around Estrella and kissed her on both cheeks. Then she backed off and looked at her. Tears appeared in her eyes.

"You are a gift from heaven, Estrella. Here I am withering away in the wilderness and suddenly my prayers have been answered. I had a dream—"

"Always she has dreams," Don Pietro cut in.

"Listen to me, Pietro," Rosita demanded, "I don't like this quiet, heavy air. The birds have all gone from the trees, and not even the rattlesnake emerges from his hole."

"Of course, of course, my dear. But our guests need attention and food. Then they will explain their presence in this isolated *pueblo*."

Rosita's eyes flashed as she picked out Mark. "Who is this gringo cowboy you expose to your daughter, Senora Martinos?"

"I'll explain all that later, Rosita. Suffice it to say he is my protector," Senora Martinos told her.

"We shall gave a proper dinner when you are refreshed.

I shall order the menu myself. Come, I personally will show you to your rooms. Perhaps the gringo would prefer the servants' quarters."

"I'll bunk with the *greasers*," Mark said pointedly. "I reckon I ain't used to high-class conversation or spiced-up food."

"Go wash up and shave, Mark," Senora Martinos said. "Beat the dust out of your clothes. You'll eat here with us. You're no peon. You're the owner of a large herd of cattle and a ranch in Arizona. You are my protector. I want you in the house near me."

"We have plenty rooms now that the children have gone," Don Pietro said.

Mark went out to the adobe stables where one of the peons had unsaddled and fed his horse. He found his soap and towel in his warbag and proceeded to wash up in the water trough. He got out a spare shirt, and after using his razor, he put it on. That was the limit of his refinement.

He felt ill at ease at the long refectory table with its white linen, but the food was excellent in spite of his former reference to it. He listened as Senora Martinos and Magdalena told about their trip so far, and why they had come along on the trying journey, and how it was decided to stop over a couple of days in Santa Barbara and get cleaned up and rested.

"Why are you taking Magdalena to America? Are not the convents at Mexico City good enough for her?" Senora Oliviera asked.

"All the royal snobs didn't die with Maximilian. There are too many of them left in Mexico City. I don't want Magdalena taken in by those fops."

"For once we agree on something, Dona Estrella. Don

Pietro insisted on sending our children to Mexico City to live with their aunt. She was married to a Maximilian loyalist. He got shot in the revolt, but she still calls herself a countess."

"She was young then," Don Pietro said. "Nobody— nobody calls her countess anymore. Let's drop the subject. I have more important things to discuss with Senor Nelson."

Mark tensed. He expected to pay some sort of bribes along the way. This was the first one. "What business is that, Don Pietro?" he asked cautiously.

"We are a poor *pueblo* here, senor, in spite of the silver. We have many peons to care for. Any cattle feeding on Santa Barbara grass, and using the pond outside the *pueblo*, must pay a reasonable fee."

Here it comes, Mark thought. He kept his brown eyes on Don Pietro's black ones. "And what fee is that, Don Pietro?"

"Two cents a day in American money, senor, for each head of cattle."

"Ain't that a mite steep, Don Pietro? I only paid two dollars a head for them cows. Two cents a day is goin' to cut me down considerable. I figure ten dollars a day for the herd is more like it."

"Everybody profits where they can, senor. The fee is two cents per head per day. We make no exceptions," Don Pietro said blandly.

"We'll move out in the morning," Mark asserted.

"You are being optimistic, senor. Even then you will have to pay for two days. I have others to think of."

"He means," Senora Oliviera said frankly, "that when a

trail herder, like Velasco, for instance, brings a herd by here, he gets a cut of the graft."

Don Pietro gave her a nasty look. "Mind your own business, Rosita. You like your fine house. But how you think I afford it?"

Mark saw no sense in haggling. The fact that Velasco might have profited by the stopover disturbed him. True, Luis had seemed reluctant to stop. But that must have been an act. What other schemes would he have to put up with before he reached the border? He finished his dinner and excused himself.

"I have to check on my drovers if I hope to move out tomorrow," he explained.

Lolita, who had listened to the conversation without joining it, rose from her chair.

"I go with you, Senor Mark."

"I'm going to the *cantina*," Mark warned her. "I can't bother with you, Lolita. You'll just get into trouble."

"I will be no bother, senor. I will sing and they will throw money to me and I will give eet to you to pay for the cattle."

Mark was touched by her offer, but he refused it. "I'm not askin' you to belittle yourself on my account, Lolita."

He went out with Lolita at his heels. Magdalena called after him, "I wish I could go with you, Mark!"

Mark intended to talk the men into cutting their celebration short so they would be able to work the herd in the morning, but if Velasco was getting a cut of the toll money, he could refuse to cooperate. Velasco had no love for him, that was sure.

Mark expected trouble at the border. He didn't know

exactly how it would come, but it would come in some form or other. He had to hold the trouble down until he got to the border. Although he had not expected Don Pietro's demands, he couldn't blame the *alcalde*. He'd been exposed to the same sort of the shenanigans back in the States: land grabbers and river-crossing bandits trying to collect tolls for all sorts of phony reasons. He'd been lucky so far. Perhaps this would be the only holdup on their way to the border.

He trudged up the dusty street with Lolita at his heels, past the faded and shabby stores and homes until he was beyond the village well. There two *cantinas* faced each other on either side of the street. Raucous sounds emanated from them and outside one of them a man was strumming a guitar while a small group about him sang a plaintive Spanish love song. Without hesitation, Lolita went over to the group and lifted her voice in clear dulcet tones. The singers stopped singing and gave her the center of the stage. A few men straggled out of the canteens to listen to her and stare at her in surprised bewilderment. It was as though she had dropped from heaven, an angel without wings. A few pesos were thrown at her feet with the cheers and applause of the men. Two women came from one *cantina* and glared at this intruder who was disrupting their business. One of them approached Lolita and berated her with threatening gestures. In her quick, no-nonsense way, Lolita punched the girl in the face.

"*Ole!*" the men shouted, hoping to see a catfight, but Mark strode over to the group and kept the girls apart.

"What's going on here, hombres?" he demanded of the men.

One of the men shrugged, pushed back his sombrero, and scratched his thick black hair. "Who knows, senor? It ees the weather. This hot, still weather make everyone restless. It ees nothing but the devil who walks the land."

Mark didn't know what the man was talking about; some native superstition no doubt.

"Lolita, you go back to the *alcalde's* house," Mark ordered.

"No, senor, I go into the *cantina* and sing. They throw pesos at me—pesos I give to you, Mark."

"I reckon there ain't many pesos in this *pueblo* to be thrown away. I don't want you getting into trouble. I've got trouble enough," Mark warned her.

The men jabbered together and one of them spoke up. "She will get in no trouble, senor. We will all take the care of her."

Mark saw the futility of argument. Lolita had shown that she could defend herself. Mark followed the group into the *cantina*, choking on the rancid smell of cigarette smoke and spilled *cerveza*. The dingy place was lit by a couple of lanterns. In the dim light the swarthy faces looked all alike. They had the agitated look of men whose liquor had already excited them. Mark recognized some of his drovers there, but he knew his orders would not be obeyed. Luis Velasco was their *jefe*, and they responded only to him. Mark couldn't see Luis among the faces. He backed out of the *cantina* before any of the crowd realized he was there and decided to make sport of the gringo. He crossed the street to the opposite *cantina* and found the light and atmosphere no better than in the one he had just left. It wasn't hard to spot Luis Velasco. He was the center of a group at the crude bar for which he was buying drinks. He could afford the cheap *cerveza* and tequila, Mark mused, out of his cut of the payoff to Don Pietro. Mark shouldered his way through the small group who looked on him with suspicion, and sidled up to Velasco.

"Something's come up, Luis," he said in an undertone.

"Hello, *amigo*! What's wrong?" Luis asked.

"It's not going very good, Luis." He went on to explain about the toll demanded by Don Pietro.

"But that ees the custom, *amigo*. You understand that, do you not?" Luis remarked with feigned surprise.

"I understand it now. We can't hang around here paying Don Pietro eighty dollars a day. We've got to move out tomorrow. You get the men together for an early morning start."

"Senor, to you I must explain the facts of life below the border," Luis said in a hard voice.

CHAPTER FOUR

Mark was disturbed by Velasco's tone of voice. His impulse was to assert his authority, but if he did so, and was flatly disobeyed, it would put him in the position of having to eat crow or face an open revolt. He knew he was taking a chance by coming six hundred miles below the border to buy cattle for two dollars a head. It was a good price. But there were other things to be considered. The temperament of the peon, for instance. They were still in a state of revolt, although Diaz, the president of Mexico, had seemed to have taken firm control of the government. A gringo was still suspect and had to rely upon the forebearance of the Mexicans rather than the protection of the law. Mark looked about the smoky, dimly lit room for sight of Teach or Nagle, but he could not see them.

"*Amigo*, perhaps you had better explain the facts of life below the border," Mark said flatly. "I seem to be ignorant of them."

"My *vaqueros* were promised a couple of days' rest in Santa Barbara. Look about you, senor. Already they are drunk. By morning they will be more drunk. If I try to stop them from drinking, they will not listen. I will lose their loyalty. Without me, you have no *vaqueros*. Without *vaqueros*, Don Pietro would have possession of the herd," Luis explained.

Mark felt his dander rising. Imprudently, he said, "Is that the only reason you want keep the herd here, Luis?"

Luis backed away from the bar, his swarthy face an inscrutable mask. "What do you mean, senor, by that remark?"

Mark couldn't hold back, although he sensed the danger. "I mean the longer the herd stays near Santa Barbara, the bigger your cut of Don Pietro's tariff will be."

Velasco's action, after hearing Mark's charge, was surprising. He let out a raucous laugh and raised his glass of tequila. "*Amigo*, I salute you. The graft you accuse me of ees not evil. It ees a way of life. Do you think Don Pietro will let you go in the morning? Or the morning after that? Or the next morning? Already he has his *vaqueros* picking out the best animals from your herd to give to the people of the town. They will eat beef again instead of jackrabbits or coyotes."

Mark felt helpless against this system. He had expected Velasco to be angry and even show physical violence at his hint of graft. Instead, he had laughed at him and labeled him a fool.

"Have you seen Dave Teach or Rex Nagle here, Luis?" he asked stiffly.

"They come here. They buy some bottles and take them with them. Perhaps they had a girl along," Luis hinted.

Twilight had given away to moonlight when Mark went outside. He looked into the *cantina* into which Lolita had vanished. She was still singing, even though the sound of voices almost drowned her out. He looked into the murk for sight of Teach and Nagle. They were tall enough to rise above the heads of Indians and Mexicans. He couldn't see them. He turned away. Let Lolita sing her heart out, if she had a heart. To try to take her out of that hovel of drunken men would result in a duplication of the fight in Nocariza. He had to find Teach and Nagle and explain the bind he was in concerning the herd of cattle. From what Velasco had told him, he could be held up here indefinitely at the will of Don Pietro, and the herd could dwindle into a mere handful not worth driving. Perhaps with sufficient bribes he could induce two or three of the *vaqueros* to help him and, with Teach and Nagle, the five of them could bunch the herd and move them out of Don Pietro's territory.

As Mark walked warily down the littered street, he remembered the women. He could not subject them to danger. After all, they were primarily Luis Velasco's responsibility. He sighed. They would all have to remain in Santa Barbara under Don Pietro's protection for the time being.

He saw the eye of a lighted cigarette and behind it a boy leaning against a post. He asked the boy if he had seen Teach and Nagle, two gringos, passing by.

"I think, senor, they have gone to the stable of the *alcalde*." The boy pointed in the direction of the stable behind Don Pietro's house.

Mark headed for the stable. It was as good a place as any to get drunk without inviting trouble. He found them on a dirt heap in the moonlight, passing a bottle back and forth.

"What the hell are you doing here, Dave?" Mark demanded.

"We couldn't stand them stinking dives in town, *amigo*. Here we have the fresh air and the moonlight. Here, have a swig of this rotgut." Teach offered him the bottle.

"No time for that. We're in trouble." He went on to explain his conversation with Luis Velasco. "Luis ain't in no hurry to get out of here so long as he's gettin' a cut of the toll charges."

"I reckon we been outsmarted, boss. A couple of days' rest won't hurt us or the herd," Nagle put in.

"It ain't that simple. Luis and Don Pietro can keep us here indefinitely. Already Don Pietro has men picking out the choice cattle to feed the people of the *pueblo*."

"He's a regular Robin Hood—rob the rich an' feed the poor. You can stand to lose three or four head of cattle, *amigo*. I ain't seen no prime beef among 'em, just whangleather an' bones."

"We could lose the whole herd. I've got most of my money an' my future tied up in that herd," Mark told them.

"You should have followed my advice," Teach said, taking a swig from the bottle. "You should've stayed in Arizona an' whangled cattle out of the brush like the other outfits done."

"There ain't no more brush cattle to be whangled outta the brush. Right after the war there was plenty of them because the herds had been neglected. Now, all them brush cattle wear brands."

"Brands can be changed, *amigo*," Teach reminded him.

"You're talking about rustlin', Dave. Rustlin' is a one-way ticket to a rope."

"You could rustle some of the cattle off your sweetheart's ranch. Old man Ford can spare a few," Nagle suggested.

"That would be a sure way to kill off everything with Delma. Ford dared me to make a start on my own before he'd sanction a marriage with his daughter, an' Delma agreed with him. Rustlin' Ford's cattle would be one sure way to queer me with Delma and her pa."

"Mebbe you could get another girl who wouldn't be so finicky about where you got your cattle," Teach suggested with a grin.

"Forget it," Mark said. "I don't see no humor in the situation."

"Sorry, *amigo*," Teach apologized. "We're with you all the way. We'll be up at the crack of light."

A puff of wind disturbed the stagnant air. It came from the direction of the Gulf of Mexico, miles to the west. It gave a promise of a cooler night.

"Well, this breeze should make things a mite more comfortable," Mark said. "I'm goin' up to the house."

"We'll sleep in the hayloft of the barn. It will be cooler than in the house," Nagle said. "After we finish this rotgut we bought. Sure you won't have a swig, Mark?"

"No. I gotta talk with Senora Martinos."

Before Mark reached the house the breeze had stopped as though a door had been closed on it, and the doldrums settled in again. He went into the house through the kitchen where the servants and cook were still cleaning up after the fancy dinner.

"Why you come this way, senor?" the buxom cook asked, her puffy face gleaming with sweat. "It is bad luck for strange hombre to come into kitchen. Vamos, pronto."

Mark went into the house and found his group, minus Lolita, talking in the parlor.

Magdalena looked up with a radiant smile as he entered. "It's about time, Mark. Where did you leave our little friend, Lolita?"

"I left her in the *cantina* where I found her in Norcariza," Mark replied.

"And who is there to defend her sacred honor?" Magdalena asked.

"I reckon she can defend herself. A dozen *amigos* are taking care that none of them take advantage of her."

"They might toss dice to see who gets her," Magdalena suggested. "Or they might even start a fight, winner take all."

"Do I detect a note of jealousy in your voice, Magdalena?" Senora Martinos chided her.

"Perhaps. A girl should be jealous of her future husband," she said brazenly.

"I've already got a girl back in Arizona waitin' to marry me," Mark warned her.

"That's a long way off, Mark Nelson. Come sit with me on the sofa and I will make you forget her."

"What unspeakable manners," Senora Oliviera said, glaring at Magdalena's mother. "Is that how you taught her?"

"Love needs no teacher. Like water it follows its natural course," Senora Martinos said with a forced smile.

"Our daughters are raised to marry men of importance, not rabble," Senora Oliviera said haughtily.

"I'm too tired to bandy words, *amigos*. What room am I to sleep in?" Mark looked at Senora Martinos, who had insisted on his protection.

"I'll show you to your room, Mark," Magdalena said, rising from the sofa. "I'm to sleep with Mother. You will be in an adjoining room to protect us."

Don Pietro said sternly, "Do you question my hospitality, *amigos*? I have no bandits on my *hacienda*. You will not be robbed or assaulted."

"Of course, Don Pietro, we understand that," Senora Martinos told him. "It's just that after such a long ride through barren country, we become uneasy in a strange house. No insult is intended."

"Come on, Mark," Magdalena said, extending her hand. "Let them haggle by themselves."

Mark took her small, smooth hand. Picking up a lamp from a pair on a table, they went into the hall and up the curved stairway. In the upstairs hall they stopped at a door.

"This room adjoins ours," Magdalena explained. She opened the door and preceded him inside.

"Didn't your mother teach you that it's wrong to be in a room alone with a strange man?" he chided her.

"By the time we get to the border, you will not be a stranger, Mark. To me you're not a stranger now. You're honest, ambitious, and not afraid to get your hands dirty. I have no love or respect for the dandies I'm supposed to marry. They live off the name of their families and lay about drinking and cheating on their wives."

Mark lit the lamp on the table by the bed. He turned a serious face on Magdalena. "Don't set your heart on impossible goals, *amiga*. By the time I get to the border, I might be a poor, red-necked cowboy. I might not be able to keep you in lace handkerchiefs."

"What do you mean by that? I hate lace handkerchiefs," she told him, pouting.

Mark told her about his talk with Velasco and the probability that Don Pietro would keep them at Santa Barbara until he had decimated the herd. "I could reach the border with nothing but cripples and dog meat. I couldn't afford a wife."

"Than I shall become a nun and preserve my love for you until I die," she said emphatically.

"Don't talk like a fool. You are too beautiful to escape from true love, and too spunky to be a nun," he told her.

"Am I not beautiful for you, Mark?"

"Look, Magdalena, you're beautiful enough for a prince or a president. Let's drop the subject," he said, looking into her upturned face. "I've got to get up at the crack of light and try to save some of my herd."

She rose on tiptoe and, with her hand behind his head, she kissed him hard on the lips. "Good night, Mark. Maybe now you will see me in your dreams."

With that she took up the lamp and walked from the room, her slim body as regal as a queen's.

Exhausted, Mark shucked his boots and Levi's, and hung his shirt on the foot of the bed. Even with the feel of Magdalena's lips still on his, he was too tired to dream. As was his habit, he woke up as dawn was breaking. He saw the lace curtain at his window blowing wildly. He heard a subdued, pulsing sound that shook his narrow window. The sound was like that of an angry beast striving to free itself from bondage. He got up warily in his underwear and went to the window. Pushing the drapes and curtain aside, he stared into the semi-darkness. What he saw more than disturbed him. It sent a shudder of fear through his lean body. This was the reason for the stagnant air and doldrums of the day before!

Gusts of wind were picking up the litter in the streets and swirling it in the air. There was a guttural sound behind the wind, and over the land toward the gulf, a black cloud loomed, shot through with flashes of lightning. For a moment he stared at the approaching storm, immobilized by the awesome threat it presented. He quickly pulled on his Levi's and boots, not bothering with his shirt. He invaded the adjoining bedroom without ceremony.

"Get up, Senora Martinos and Magdalena! Hell's breaking loose outside!"

The two women sat up. They looked at him with surprise and fear.

"What are you doing in our bedroom, Mark?" the senora demanded.

"Protecting you, senora. Soon we'll be in the center of hell. A hurricane's comin' at us!"

"We haven't had a hurricane on the west coast for years!" Senora Martinos claimed.

"There's one here now. It must've played hell in Baja, and come straight in from the gulf. Listen!"

They held their breaths for a moment and heard the intermittent, snarling gusts.

"*Madre de Dios,* you are right, Mark Nelson! It could sweep this town off the face of the earth!"

"Get dressed and stay downstairs. If the roof blows off it won't harm you there. I've got to go out and warn the people," Mark said, breathing hard.

He rushed downstairs as the weird howling outside increased. He went through the servants' quarters, shouting a warning. Most of them were already up. Some boys were building a fire in the big fireplace on which the cooking was done. He stopped them, pouring water on the fire they had started.

"No fire. The big wind is coming. It could burn the house down." He found the fat cook. "Keep everyone in the lower part of the house. This wind can raise plenty hell with everything!" He went out the back door just in time to see the upper part of the stable above the adobe walls tear loose and ride the wind like a kite. He wondered where Teach and Nagle were. Had they gone down to the herd? At the moment the herd didn't matter. People were going to die; many people. In the street he saw the dogs skulking in holes or in clumps of chaparral behind the adobe houses. At the upper end of the street the silver cross on top of the church was swinging wildly. Frightened people were crouching outside their homes. Many were running for the protection of the church.

Mark yelled as he ran among them, "Go to the mine, go inside the tunnel!"

At the *cantinas*, drunken men were sleeping, drugged by the slop they had consumed the night before. He kicked some of them, but they merely grunted and stayed where they were. He had no time to waste with them. He wondered where Lolita was. He couldn't find her among the drunks, nor did he expect to. The wind was changing now to a deafening roar. It blotted out the dawn, giving the scene a gray translucence. People were fighting the wind, trying to get to the church, but they were blown back like chips in a maelstrom. The wind clutched greedily at every projection, every bush, even the mud-thatched roofs of the adobe houses. It snatched them away like a giant playing an evil game.

There were women in the road lying on top of their babies. In the murky light Mark saw Luis Velasco, his dark hair blowing in the wind, risking his life to pull victims from the rubble of their collapsed huts. Mark reached him.

"This is pure hell, Luis!" Mark yelled above the tumult. "I told the people to go to the mine. Some of them will make it!"

"*Si, amigo*. The others go to the church. Always they go to the church. They cling to the benevolence of a God they know nothing of but what the *padre* has taught them. Sometimes the church crumbles."

"You're right, Luis. When that swinging cross falls on the roof of the church, it could go right through," Mark said.

He studied the church. The dome in the center made of brick could collapse and kill those beneath it.

"Where is Lolita?" Mark asked.

"She go to the church to quiet the people!" Luis yelled.

Mark fought his way toward the church, crawling on hands and knees at times to keep from being blown away. The screaming of the people, mingled with the horrible sounds of the wind, formed a bedlam in his head that blocked out all sanity. He struggled like a mechanical man, aware of the fury about him, but apart from it mentally. His movements were those of an insect, crushed but not dead, that squirms for the last dregs of life for no apparent reason.

He had been in a hurricane in Texas years before, when the wind screeching in off the sea brought great waves that wiped out the colony that had started on a nearby low island. A lot of people had died in that holocaust of wind, rain, and fires ignited by overturned stoves. He had no thought of giving up.

There was a lull in the wind, and in the murk about him Mark saw a naked baby in the road, screaming its lungs out. It was held there by a barrier of adobe bricks. He picked up the screaming child and tucked it under one arm. The church was just ahead of him.

CHAPTER FIVE

His hair straggling over his eyes and his shirt torn to shreds, Mark stumbled into the church. His stout Levi's were still belted about his slim waist. The baby under his arm had stopped crying, either exhausted or comforted by the arm that held it. He looked about, bleary-eyed. He forced the door shut with one hand, and the quiet in the place was astounding. Little sound of the outside fury came through the thick walls. There were no windows in the church, only one round hole above the altar. The hole was on the leeward side of the church so none of the wind entered it. Someone had lit the candles on the altar, and clustered about the altar rail, like bees around their queen, were the people praying with the *padre*. Lolita saw Mark, and came over, gently taking the child from his arm. Her face was streaked with tears but her voice was steady.

"What is it, Mark? What does it mean?" she pleaded.

"It's a hurricane, *amiga*—a bad wind that destroys everything in its path. There hasn't been one in this location since before you were born. It will die out, leaving death and destruction behind it."

Crooning to the baby, she sat on one of the crude benches that served as pews. "What have the people of Santa Barbara done to deserve this punishment, Mark?" she whimpered.

"It's no punishment, *amiga*," he assured her. "Nature plays her tricks on the just and the unjust alike, I reckon. There ain't no way to stop it. You put up with it or you die with it."

Mark looked up at the roof of the church. Already mortar was sifting down from around the edges of the dome. The people had to be moved from the center of the church before the dome collapsed.

"Give the baby to one of the women, Lolita. We've got to get these people away from the altar, back against the walls or into the baptismal."

"They will not go, Mark. They put their faith in the *padre* and the cross," Lolita said.

"If the dome falls, they'll all be killed. We gotta make them understand," Mark insisted. "Speak to them in Spanish, *amiga*. I'll do what I can."

Mark worked his way through the tightly packed mass to the side of the *padre*. "Father, tell the people to disperse. Tell them to get against the walls or in the corners."

"Why do you say this, my son? The Lord is here, in the tabernacle. He will answer their prayers," the priest demurred.

"He can answer them better if they stay alive, Father. If the dome collapses, they will be killed," Mark explained.

"I would be of little faith if I stopped their prayers and told them to hide in the corners," the priest intoned.

Ignoring the priest, Mark harangued the people, pushing them toward the rear, shouting in broken Spanish for them to disperse into the safer places. Lolita added her voice to his entreaties. Some of the people looked up at the dome. It was still there. They doubted Mark's warning. Mark persuaded some of the men to help him break up the knot of women and children who put their trust in the *padre*. Slowly they moved the people away from the altar back against the rear walls and other safer sections of the church. The *padre* stayed on the altar holding his crucifix and intoning prayers that were drowned out by the chatter and the protests of the people. One old woman squirmed out of the crowd and went back to kneel before the priest, her faith unshakable. Mark pushed the people to the wall. Some of them he had kneel under the stout benches that served as pews. The mortar was sifting faster from between the bricks. Mark straightened up, sweat pouring off him. He glared through the dim light toward the altar. Just as he was starting back to drag the old woman away from the altar, there was a loud thud on the roof. The crucifix had fallen! Almost simultaneously, the dome collapsed! It crashed down in a rain of mortar and bricks upon the altar and the area before it. He had gotten the people away from danger just in time; all but the priest and the faithful woman who had knelt before him. The priest had been struck down by the first of the bricks and now lay under a pile of rubble in company with the old woman.

A cry of lamentation went up from the people at the sight of the tragedy. Mark craned his neck to see if there was more danger above. The wind roared through the big hole in the roof adding a raucous snarl of derision to their agony. Their *padre* was dead. Whom could they turn to now?

Mark cried at the men, "Give me a hand. We've gotta uncover the *padre* and the old woman!"

"The devil do this thing! If we go there, we, too, will die!" they insisted.

"The devil had nothing to do with it, *amigos*! The dome was not built to withstand such force!" Mark told them.

Lolita came forward. "I will help you, Mark. Perhaps the *padre* is still alive. These pigs have the courage of a louse."

Some of the men, shamed by her outburst, came forward. Mark himself was not sure how long the rest of the roof would last, but an effort had to be made to rescue the priest. They dug into the rubble with their bare hands, tossing the bricks aside. They reached the old woman first. She was dead, her hands still clutching her rosary.

"Take her back and let the women take care of her," Mark ordered.

He and the others went back to working on the bricks. With the roar of the storm, the weeping of the women, and their incantations, it was like toiling in a remote corner of hell. The *padre* was buried under the center of the pile of bricks. They had to be careful in removing the bricks. If the *padre* was still alive, they might compound his injuries. The pile of bricks dwindled and soon they uncovered part of the priest's black cassock. Next they had the crucifix and his hands uncovered. His head followed. By some quirk of fate, some bricks had come together on end forming an arch that partly protected his head. His lips moved slightly, intoning a word in Latin.

The group of men, their hands folded tightly, exclaimed, "It ees a miracle!"

Mark had no faith in miracles. He knelt beside the priest and spoke in his ear. "Are you all right, Father?"

There was a moment of tense silence and then the priest's voice, barely more than a whisper, said, "I am alive, my son. That is all I know. You were right in forcing the people away from this danger."

"Never mind that. Can you move your head?"

The priest's skeletal head nodded and turned. His burning eyes, irritated by the mortar, stared owlishly at Mark. "I can move my head. My breath comes with difficulty. My chest, my chest..." His voice trailed off.

Mark goaded the men. "Clear the bricks away from him."

Mark with the help of two of the men lifted the priest's emaciated form and carried it to the back of the church. The women who still had their shawls and the men with serapes spread them on the stone tiles of the floor to make a bed for the *padre*. No sooner was this done than there was a knocking on the door of the church. Mark attempted to open the door and keep control of it, but the wind, snarling in through the hole in the roof, clamped it shut. Mark asked for help. Three of the men forced the door inward far enough for a person to enter. Through the opening came a bedraggled figure. There was no mistaking her calling. The shreds of a wimple hung from the band about her shaven head. Her robe was in tatters, held together by the heavy chain of beads about her waist.

"I am the only nun here to teach the children. I come from the school behind the church. I found on my way people who needed my prayers."

She was a youngish woman, her features unlined and with a beauty reflected from within.

"We have someone here who could use your prayers, Sister," Mark told her. He explained what had happened.

"I have no instruments, senor, but prayer," she told Mark. She knelt beside the prostrate form of the priest and brushed the hair back from his forehead. The touch of her small, cool hand aroused the holy man.

"Sister Inez, you are still alive," he murmured.

"Si, si, padre. Do not extend yourself. Where does it hurt most?"

He motioned to his chest.

Sister Inez opened the top part of his robe and bared his chest. "What sign is this?" she said, pointing to the imprint of the crucifix upon his skin.

"He was holding a crucifix in his hands when he was struck. I reckon that caused the imprint," Mark explained.

"Perhaps," she said. "Also perhaps it is a stigmata, immortalizing him."

Mark had no time to differ with her opinion. "Will he live?"

"Get me some cloth soaked in cold water," Sister Inez ordered.

"There ees no water in the church, Sister," a woman informed her.

"Soak the cloth in the baptismal fount," she told them.

There was a momentary lull in the wind. Mark found Lolita, who was a picture of exhaustion, quieting the babies and doing what she could for those battered and bruised by the storm.

"I'm going to see if I can make it down to Don Pietro's house. This lull in the wind might turn into more fury than we had up to now," he told her. "You'd better get some rest, *amiga*."

"In a hell, there is no rest, Mark, only suffering." In a sudden burst of emotion, she put her arms around him and buried her head on his shoulder. A convulsive sob shook her slim body.

Mark pressed her to him, his emotion matching her own. Her courage impelled him to put a hand under her chin and turn her tear-stained face up. With a fervor that surprised even him, he pressed his lips upon hers. It was like flint to steel igniting a fire in his blood. He let her go gently, shaken by the experience. For the moment he had forgotten Delma Ford.

"Thank you, Mark Nelson. I have been kissed many times, but this time I will remember," she said.

Mark picked her up and carried her to one of the benches. "You stay here and rest, *amiga*. Let the others help each other. I've gotta go before the wind starts up bad again."

"*Vaya con Dios*, Mark," she whispered as she closed her eyes.

Outside, Mark found the wind had quieted, but it was

still strong. He was going with the wind and it was all he could do to keep on his feet by digging in the high heels of his boots. Swept forward by the wind, he reached Don Pietro's *hacienda* in short order. The trees that protected the house were still there but their branches were shredded and broken. The lower half of the stable still stood against the onslaught. There was a huddle of people inside the structure. Mark didn't stop at the stable. He went through the detached kitchen and found it a shambles. The fat cook was lying in the debris, a wound on her head indicating she had been struck by some flying object. She had no doubt stopped here to protect her precious kettles and pots, coveted things in this primitive village. He bent over her. She was still alive. He tried to move her, pull her into the house. She was a dead weight that defied his efforts. He fought his way back to the stable and found the people huddled there mumbling prayers, stupefied by the fury that had come upon them. He persuaded two men to help him carry the cook into the house. The men complied under protest. When they had the injured cook laid out on the dining-room floor, Mark bid them to help themselves to what food they could find in the shattered kitchen as a reward to share with the others in the stable.

Mark was so engrossed with saving the cook, he was unaware of what was going on around him. When he looked up he was amazed and curious. People were seated like dumb zombies against the walls, under the heavy refectory table, and skulking behind the velvet drapes. The dining room was miraculously spared up to now. The upper floor of the big house was still intact. The refugees looked at him with wide, frightened eyes. Mark moved into the parlor. There he was confronted by a scene that fascinated and amazed him. The beautiful salon had been turned into a hospital. Magdalena was changing a diaper on a whimpering baby. Senora Oliviera was bandaging a woman's arm. Senora Martinos was putting splints on a boy's leg with the help of a young girl. The place reeked. Don Pietro was rushing about helping wherever he could.

For a moment Mark stood immobile, touched by the scene before him. There were no aristocrats now, no peons, only people helping people. Magdalena raised her eyes and saw him.

"Thank God, thank God, you're safe, Mark. I envisioned you struck down in the street being a good Samaritan. I prayed for you," she told him.

"I reckon I had some weird ideas about you. I figured the house might have collapsed and drove you all out into the storm," Mark said.

"The walls of the house are thick, Mark. The weight of the rubble above has held the floor in place above us. Where have you been, Mark?"

He told her about the tragedy at the church. "Nature takes everything in its path, in spite of God's benevolence. The *cantina* was still standing the last time I saw it."

"Sometimes the devil wins out, Mark. Eventually, all things are evened out."

"It's evened out for the poor beggars who are buried under the rubble, or hurled to their death through the air. What can I do here, *amiga*?"

Before Magdalena could answer, Rex Nagle came from the hall door carrying the bloody body of a child, while the mother clung to his arm. Mark was shocked by his appearance.

"Well, I'll be damned!" Mark exclaimed. "Where did you come from, Rex? I figured you an' Teach was blowed over the mountains all the way to the Chihuahua."

"We was blowed away with the hay, Mark—landed on top of it," Rex said, surrendering the stricken child to Magdalena.

"Where's Teach?"

"He's on his way to the border."

"You mean he ran out?"

"No, he ain't run out. He'd been in a hurricane in Louisiana once. There wasn't much left after the blow. He figured these people here was goin' to need food, medicine, an' clothes. We managed to crawl back to the stable. He saddled a horse an' took off through the storm for the border."

"He'll never make it, Rex. The storm ain't over."

"He'll ride it out, Mark. He may kid around a lot, but he's tough inside. Bisbee and Douglas are the nearest towns where he can get enough help to do any good. I stayed behind to do what I can here. I ain't welcome in the States. I figure when the wind lets up we can gather a few of your scattered steers to feed these people."

"Rex, I didn't know you were a missionary at heart," Mark said.

"Will one of you men help me with that old man in the corner? We've got to move him. I think his leg is broken. We'll have to set it as best we can, and improvise some splints," Magdalena told them.

"I'll help you, ma'am," Rex said promptly.

"Call me Magdalena, Rex. There's no time for formality here."

Mark watched them go. Rex Nagle with his thick black Indian hair and his heavy black eyebrows looked Spanish enough to be a native. Mark sought out Don Pietro, who was resting from his assorted labors.

"Are there any stored-up provisions in the town, Don Pietro?" he inquired.

Don Pietro looked at him, his aristocratic face lined with fatigue. "There is some corn in the brick storehouse, if it hasn't been blown away. There are some provisions in the trading post that can be dug out even if the building is blown down. There has been no rain to ruin them."

Mark knew there would be rain following the storm, torrential rain, but he didn't mention this to Don Pietro. "Dave Teach, my *segundo* has gone on the road to the border, hoping to bring back supplies and clothing."

"The devil-wind will blow him down before he goes a kilometer, *amigo*."

"Don't underestimate a range rider, senor. Blizzards and floods are to be endured. By the time this lull in the wind is over, he'll be on the fringe of the storm area."

"But it will take days to get the supplies down here," Don Pietro protested.

"Days that we'll have to endure. Many people are in the mine," Mark reminded him. "They will be strong and rested when they come out. They can help dig out the supplies and the dead. There are some horses still in the stable. If necessary we can butcher them."

"My prize *caballos*?" Don Pietro lamented. "That will be a sacrifice too painful to be endured."

"Think what the others are enduring, senor. The horses can be replaced, but the people must eat."

Tears streamed down Don Pietro's proud face. Mark didn't know what he was crying over—the peons, the horses, or himself.

Mark headed for the stable to see if everything was intact. First he went into the dining room and found the fat cook lying uncovered on the floor where they had dragged her. She was dead. The peons around the wall kept their eyes averted from the body. Mark took the tablecloth off the refectory table and covered the body. Then he went out to the shattered kitchen. He found the stable intact. The refugees crowded there were munching oats out of the horses' feed bin. They were better off than most. The two thoroughbred horses were restless in their stalls. Satisfied that the stable would ride out the storm, he went back to the house. He sought out Senora Martinos.

"I reckon you women are doin' a good job here. I aim to go back to the church and see if everything is all right there," he told her above the howling of the wind.

"Be careful, Mark," she cautioned him. "We'll need you here when this blows over."

He saw Magdalena and Rex involved in their work, so he didn't disturb them. He went into the street. The trading post had collapsed, but the supplies would be safe as long as it didn't rain. Then the wind struck again with renewed fury as he neared the one *cantina* that was still standing. Fighting against the wind's increased force, he crawled into the *cantina*.

CHAPTER SIX

As Dave Teach headed northeast, away from Santa Barbara, he hung low over the saddle, his sombrero hanging down his back. His tousled red hair whipped about his head. He kept his horse's rump to the wind as much as possible. The wind pushed them along. The horse, one of Don Pietro's Arabians, with long legs, a lean flank, and a sturdy chest, was the offspring of horses used to the desert and its capricious sandstorms. Teach knew that his efforts might prove futile but he had to make a try. The push of the wind spared his horse a lot of effort. All he had to do was keep on his feet and let the wind hurl him along.

Teach, his bandana over his mouth and nose to keep out the dust, tried to do some thinking as he sped along.

How in the living hell did he get into the position that he found himself? He had been a carefree expatriate, living by his wits: gambling, breaking horses, or even entering a bull fight or two to make ends meet. Because of his red hair and his genial personality, he was a favorite with the senoritas. He passed off insults with a twinkle of his blue eyes, using his fists only when there was no milder way. Now he was caught up in the tragedy of a small *pueblo* he had never heard of before. He'd been tricked by loyalty to a friend; a friend who had the glib tongue of a dreamer and the hope of getting rich off cattle that were skin and bones. Now even the skin and bones were gone with the wind.

Teach calculated his chances of getting help to the *pueblo* before the people were starved into eating grass and cactus pulp. With the wind facing him he would have little chance of reaching the border in time, but with the wind at his back he could make the settlement of Douglas in two and a half days. It would take the wagons at least four days on the road to bring the relief supplies. It was a dismal prospect, but the only one with a chance of success. There was no communication with Santa Barbara except by horseback, and the Mexican towns close enough to it would have few supplies to spare in that starvation land. A lull in the wind gave him a chance to let his horse get a breather. He drank some of the water from the canteen he had brought along and, pouring the remainder into his sombrero, he let the horse drink it all. As he mounted to ride on, through some low hills, the wind came back with renewed force. The storm had reduced visibility to less than a hundred yards and with night coming on what little light there was faded rapidly. He topped the summit of a hill and below him he saw a small valley through which ran a stream. The hills apparently forced the wind up above the valley and on the stream he saw a ranch with two adobe buildings and corrals containing some livestock.

With a surge of relief he headed for the outpost. It was dusk when he reached it. Some mangy dogs, snarling and barking, surrounded his horse. He shouted above the noise of the wind and the dogs, "Hello the house!"

Two surly-looking men came out, one carrying a rifle and the other with a lantern. Teach felt disturbed by their appearance, but he had to stop for water and perhaps a change of mounts. The thoroughbred, despite his breeding, was exhausted.

"*Buenas tardes*, senors," Teach said in as friendly a voice as he could muster.

The men spoke in Spanish, their eyes glowing in the lantern light. "What you want here, hombre?" they asked gruffly.

In his stilted Spanish, Teach explained about the wind and why he was riding north. The men digested his words, their grim manner softening.

"We have the robbers come here. They take what little we have. If you are not a thief, where did you find that excellent horse?"

"It belongs to Don Pietro Oliviera. The bad wind scattered most of the livestock. The horse is dead tired, I am dead tired. May we stop here for a few hours, senors?"

"Your *caballo* will not rest in so short a time, senor."

"I'll leave him here and take one of your fresh horses,

senor. When I come back this way, I'll pick him up and leave your horse," Teach explained.

"In the meantime, if the *bandidos* come, they will steal this fine horse," the taller Mexican said. "What you do then?"

Teach knew he would never see the horse again. When they heard him coming they would hide the Arabian in the chaparral and vow that *bandidos* had stolen him. He was in no position to argue.

"You'll not be held responsible, senor," Teach assured him.

So the horse was rubbed down, fed some corn and wild hay that had been cut along the stream, and Teach went into the small house. The smoky air smelled of broiling meat, hung over the fire in the smoking fireplace, and of corn cakes baking on the hot stones. They offered him homemade mescal, which he refused. On his empty stomach it would explode. He ate ravenously of the food, and the atmosphere became more congenial as the meal progressed. Here they were evidently on the fringe of the storm, having escaped most of the fury of the hurricane. Teach explained the havoc the storm had wrought in Santa Barbara and why he was heading for Douglas to send back supplies. The two men and the Indian wife of one of them expressed concern for the people but had little good to say about Don Pietro.

"He steal the silver from the mine that belongs to the people. He work them hard for a few centavos a day. For him we have no love, senor, but for the peons our heart bleeds."

Teach slept on the floor near the fireplace. He fell into a drugged sleep, and when he awoke it was daylight.

"You should have kicked me awake, senora," he told the Indian woman who was bustling about the room.

"You will ride more better, senor, now that you are rested. Eat your breakfast. You will ride better on a full stomach."

Teach ate the jerky and hardtack the woman gave him. At the corral he found the two men. In the clear light of day they looked less sinister. They had his saddle with a full canteen on a staunch cow pony.

"This *caballo* will take you far, senor. Fear not for Don Pietro's *caballo*. He will be safe here."

Teach left with their *"Vaya con Dios!"* ringing in his ears.

On the morning of the third day, Teach arrived in Douglas. The town was familiar to him. Nothing had changed since he had fled across the border to escape a false charge of murder. There were the same stores with their grimy windows, the saloons with idle patrons lolling in the sun. There were some loiterers around the entrance to Crazy Joe's Bar, who stared at him. One of the loiterers came forward. He was a wide-shouldered man in a flannel shirt and warped chaps. Teach recognized him as Benny Cold, a cowpoke he had ridden with on a couple of cattle drives. He had always been friendly.

"Ain't you Dave Teach?" Benny asked.

"I reckon so, Ben."

"Where you been? We couldn't find you. Flathead

Stoker got shot in a gunfight. Afore he died he confessed it was him who killed Ted Ricker, not you. Your shot went wild. You look whipped, man. What you need is a drink. Then you can explain what brought you here. There ain't been no bounty posters on you for two years."

"So Mark told me, Ben. I just came from the backyard of hell, *amigo*." Teach went on to explain about the hurricane and the doomed town of Santa Barbara. In his excitement he raised his voice so that it carried across the room and even through the open door of Magradero's cafe adjoining the bar. The men crowded about asking questions.

"How in the hell did you get stuck there?" one man asked.

Teach told them about Mark Nelson's attempt to drive cheap Mexican cattle across the border and get a head start on a range herd.

"The danged fool oughta know better than that. Them cows could bring a disease with 'em that could wipe out our herds," another man warned.

"The cattle are whangleather an' bone, but they ain't diseased. That's beside the point. The natives in Santa Barbara are dying, some are dead. Some are crippled. The church dome fell in. I don't know whether the *padre* is dead or alive. I rode hell for breakfast up here to get some supplies to tide 'em over."

"Why should we put ourselves out for them greasers?" a man asked harshly.

"Because them greasers are human beings—women an' babies. Some of them are aristocrats, down there. Don Pietro and his wife Rosita; Magdalena, daughter of Jose

Martinos in Nocariza, and Don Jose's wife, Dona Estrella."

"Let the aristocrats get their hands dirty and help the victims," a man insisted.

"Don Pietro has turned his half-ruined house into a hospital. He's doing all kinds of dirty work hisself. His wife and Martinos's women are blood up to their elbows taking care of the injured. But they need food and they need clothing. This is the nearest place to find supplies to tide 'em over until help can come from Guadalajara."

"Why don't they eat Mark Nelson's dogies?"

"Sure," another man seconded the suggestion. "They're used to stringy beef. That is, when they can get it."

"Mark's herd is scattered all across the range!" Teach retorted with a spurt of anger.

A man came in from the cafe. He was a tall man with shaggy hair and dark eyes under overhanging brows. Teach recognized him as Doby Evers, a pushy man expanding his range and his herd by any means, fair or foul. His cheeks were sunken and his prominent chin gave his long face a horsey appearance. His checked flannel shirt stretched tightly across his arched chest.

"What's this I hear about Mark Nelson bringing in Mex cattle to stock his range?" he asked in a deceptively quiet voice.

"That's the general idea, Evers," Teach said, "but I ain't here to discuss that."

"There ain't goin' to be no discussion," Evers said. "Mark's got less'n twenty days to get cattle on his government lease or he'll lose his option an' I'm in line for the first chance at it. I need all the land I can get this side of the Chiricahua. He'll never get back in time to clinch his lease. I need the land now."

"You aimin' to steal it?" Teach dared him.

"What business is that of yours? Too bad somebody didn't collect that ransom on your head afore Flathead Stoker took the blame. I still ain't rightly sure who killed Ted Ricker," Evers said flatly.

"Take the matter of the range up with Mark when he gets here," Teach suggested.

"He may never get here, Dave," Evers said prophetically.

"Why? You goin' to send your gunhawks across the line to make sure, Doby?" Teach needled the big man.

Evers glowered at him. "Everything in its time, Dave. Right now, I'll chip in on those welfare supplies an' furnish a wagon an' team to help haul 'em down to the *pueblo*."

Teach was caught off guard by the offer. He had not expected such a magnanimous offer from Doby Evers. If Evers had an ulterior motive in making the offer Teach couldn't see what it was, unless it would give his crew a chance to delay Mark's progress to the border. Before he could muster a proper reply to Evers's offer, another man came in through the cafe door. He matched Evers in height but he lacked Evers's bulk. He was a slim man, light on his feet. Teach recognized him as Dale Ford, Delma Ford's father.

"I heard what's goin' on in here," Ford said. "Come into the cafe, Teach, and we'll talk about it."

Teach downed the drink that stood before him and followed Ford into the familiar dining room. Ma Ready was still there with her red hair done up in a bun on the back of her head. Magradero, who had started the cafe, died of mescal poisoning five years ago. Ma Ready took over the cafe but never bothered to change the name. The cafe smelled of cooking, warm bread, and steaming coffee. Ma's daughter, Pamela, blonde and blue-eyed, had grown into quite a woman since Teach had last seen her.

"Well, look what the cat dragged in. I thought that by now you'd have a Mexican wife and a couple of babies," she chided him.

Teach thought of Lolita Sanchez helping the victims of the hurricane in Santa Barbara. "Almost, Pam. Reckon I got a senorita waiting for me." He grinned. "You've grown up to be a blue-eyed doll, honey. You must drive the boys wild."

"*Boys,* yes," she said with pique. "*Boy,* no."

"Bring plenty of food for this hombre, Pam," Dale Ford cut in. "We got serious talkin' to do."

At a table near the back of the room to which Ford led him, Teach saw Delma Ford. At first glance he was befuddled by her appearance. She wasn't pretty like Pamela in her blonde frilly way. Delma's beauty had a deeper glow that gave an inner light to her regular features—her high cheekbones, her probing brown eyes, and her full-lipped mouth that seemed ready to smile or frown or remain neutral as the circumstances prescribed. Her shiny brown hair fell about her face like a halo, though he felt sure she would resent the comparison should she hear it. She used no paint or powder on her features. They didn't need it.

Her lips decided to smile as she looked up at him. "You're Red Teach, aren't you? I remember when you took off for the border with a lynch mob on your heels."

"Pardon me, miss. You must be Delma Ford, Mark Nelson's girl. That was no lynch mob after me. That was my friends biddin' me a fond farewell." Teach grinned.

"I've seldom seen such devoted friends," Delma quipped. "They seemed to be intent on keeping you home and furnishing you with a hemp necktie. You didn't notice me then. A few years can make a lot of difference in a girl."

"Them few years done real proud on you, Miss Ford," Red said gallantly.

"Sit down, Red," Dale Ford suggested. "You can talk with Delma later. Her an' me ain't on speakin' terms. She blames me for sendin' Mark below the border to buy beef. I did no such thing. I just asked him to make a start, prove his mettle before I allowed Delma to marry him. In fact, she agreed it was a good idea. She didn't want to marry a trail drover."

"You let him go into Mexico, hoping he wouldn't come back," Delma said sharply.

"I let him go because I approved of his idea. He could buy cattle across the border for pennies on the dollar and build up a herd much sooner that way. He was doin' it for you, Delma. I know how love can gnaw at a man's bones. I was young once."

"I'm young now, Pa," Delma said. "I don't want to die

an old maid waiting to be queen of the rancho. You an' Ma worked together and you've done real well. It killed Ma, but you're tall in the saddle."

"That's a rotten thing to say, girl," Dale objected. "Your ma died of tick fever. I had nothing to do with that."

"I'm sorry, Pa. My temper got the best of me," Delma apologized.

"Let it ride, honey." Ford turned his attention to Red. "I heard some disturbin' talk through the open door to the barroom. What was it all about?"

Teach told him the story from the beginning. He spared no details in picturing the havoc the hurricane had wrought on the *pueblo* of Santa Barbara. "The houses have their roofs blown off. Some of the houses collapsed, burying the people inside. The church was still standing when I managed to ride before the wind. There's dead people to be buried, injured people to be cared for, and women and children to be fed and clothed. Some of them had the clothes torn off their backs. Some of the people made their way to the silver mine. They should be safe. When I left there was no letup in the storm. If the rains follow the storm, there won't be much to salvage."

"My God!" Ford exclaimed.

"What about Mark?" Delma asked, her eyes wide.

"He was in the big house with the women."

"What women?"

Teach told her about the women on the cattle drive.

"Women on a cattle drive?" Delma asked. "How quaint."

Ruffled by the tone of Delma's voice, Teach went on to

explain about Magdalena being sent along under the protection of Luis Velasco and his *vaqueros*, to enter the convent of San Xavier near Elfrida.

"There's no time to sit here and blabber. Finish your dinner, Red. You, Delma, go to the women in the town and gather whatever clothes they can spare. I'll go to the stores and buy whatever I can and have it put on my account. You, Red, go with one of my men and pick up a freight wagon at the ranch. Have the wheels greased and hook up a four-horse team. It's going to take a number of days to get to Santa Barbara even if the trail isn't washed out," Dale Ford said like a man used to giving orders.

CHAPTER SEVEN

After a hectic day of preparation, gathering stores and clothing, and loading the wagons for their long journey, the cavvy was ready to hit the trail. Evers provided a Conestoga, one of the prairie schooners used by so many on their trek West. Beside the driver of the wagon, he was sending along three guards. Teach felt uneasy about the guards. The thought recurred to him that Evers might try to make sure that Mark wouldn't reach the border before his lease had expired, if at all. To voice his suspicions would start a controversy and delay the start of the trip. Teach submerged his suspicions. Mark could take care of any coup that Evers had planned and the supplies were desperately needed in the stricken town. Dale Ford was furnishing a sturdy freight wagon and he cannily sent along four riders beside the driver.

"You can never tell what might happen to this cargo. If the bandits, or the Indians, or even a band of Comancheros get wind of it, you'll have a runnin' fight on your hands. Besides, Mark will need help roundin' up the cattle if there are any left."

"I reckon there'll be enough men along to handle any trouble," Evers said evenly.

Or cause trouble, Teach thought. Mark could use all the loyal drovers he could get. What Luis Velasco and his *vaqueros* meant to do when the herd reached the border, no one knew but Luis himself.

Teach ignored the possibilities and addressed himself to the problem at hand. "I reckon I'll ride on ahead, an' let Mark and the others know that you're on your way. It'll give them a glimmer of hope. You men take the trail west of Agua Prieta, and follow the Yaqui River south until you come to the *pueblo*. I made it in three days coming north. It'll take you a bit longer to make it with the wagons. This ain't exactly a charity trip. I'm sure that Don Pietro will reward you with silver when the mine gets goin'."

The sun was just rising when the cavvy started out. Teach rode on ahead with a fresh mount. The cow pony he had borrowed at the isolated rancho was tied on the back of the freight wagon. Teach had told the driver to exchange it for the thoroughbred if possible. He wanted no encumbrance to slow him up on his trip south. News of the provisions on the way would bolster the spirits of the townspeople. Teach was well ahead of the wagons when he heard galloping hooves behind him. He stiffened in the saddle wondering what sort of trouble was overtaking him. A soft voice was calling to him. His pulse quickened. It was the voice of Delma Ford!

"What in heaven's name are you doin' here, Delma?" Teach demanded, slowing his pace.

"I'm going with you, Red," she said, riding alongside of him.

"Oh, no, you're not. Does your father know about this?"

"What difference would that make? I'd go in spite of him. I want to be with Mark. I'm partly responsible for sending him across the border."

Teach gave her as hard a look as he could muster. She was dressed for the trip, all right. She wore leather chaps over her California pants, plus a flannel shirt and a faded red bandana about her smooth, tanned throat. Her flat-crowned sombrero was secured under her stubborn chin with rawhide thongs. She was an appealing picture, a girl of the Golden West. He felt a small jab of panic at the idea of the two of them riding together for the next three days. For the moment he envied Mark Nelson and wondered how Mark had been able to leave her behind.

"Your pa will raise hell when he hears about this. We gotta sleep out two or three nights. It'll be hotter than a stove lid in the daytime. At night it will be cold and dangerous. A hungry puma won't ask your age or sex. He'll help hisself to the tender meat."

"If you're trying to scare me off, Red Teach, you can stop right now. I've got my own bedroll, my own gun, and my own knife if it comes to infighting. I'm sure I can be as much help in the *pueblo* as Mark's other women," she said smugly.

"What other women of his?" Teach taunted her.

"All those women you mentioned. Magdalena and Estrella and whoever."

"If you're goin' down there with a chip on your shoulder, get it off. It's pure blood, death, an' hell down there. There's a girl you didn't mention."

"Oh?"

"Yes, a singer from the *cantina* at Nocariza. She's probably up to her elbows in blood by now. Her name's Lolita. Mark beat up a feller who tried to brutalize her."

"I'm sure she was grateful. Is that why she's tagging along with the trail drive—to show her loyalty?"

"Delma, I figured you for a straight-shooter. Right now you're puttin' doubts in my mind. If you aim to be catty, save it for the women. If you don't cry real tears when you see them, Mark would be better off rid of you," Red said grimly.

She broke down at his castigation. She rode close to him and put her gloved hand on his arm. Tears welled up in her eyes. "I'm sorry I was witchy, Red. I've been under a strain since Mark left his ranch. I not only felt guilty for letting him go, instead of eloping with him to Bisbee or Nogales, I dreamed of him getting killed or falling for some enchanting senorita. Was he hurt bad in the fight in the *cantina* at Nocariza?"

"He took some hard licks, but he managed to give back more'n he took. He knocked the wind out of Velasco with the heel of his boot. Then he made the mistake of turning his back. Velasco tried to stick a knife in Mark, but it skidded off a bone. Mark pole-axed him with the butt of his gun."

"He didn't kill him?"

"Mark's no killer, Delma. When Velasco sobered up, he apologized. He turned out to be Don Jose's *jefe*, boss of the drive."

"That's kind of complicated, isn't it, Red?"

"On account of Dona Estrella and her daughter, who Don Jose put in his hands for safety, Velasco won't start nothin' on the drive until we reach the border," Red assured her.

"How's Mark? Did his cut heal?"

"He was took care of by Lolita's mother. He's all right."

Delma was silent for a while. Teach had his own thoughts. He had not expected to be riding alone with Mark Nelson's girl. The thought of it disturbed him. The nights would be long, cold, and possibly dangerous. As if he didn't have enough trouble without Delma!

They camped in the bottom of a dry barranca the first night so that their small fire of mesquite roots would not be seen. Delma made coffee and warmed up some sliced beef she had brought along. The biscuits were still tender. Teach savored the food which he would never have provided by himself. Jerky and hardtack would have sustained him on the trail. They reminisced about their lives as they watched the fire die down.

"My father wanted a boy," Delma confessed. "Instead, he got me. My mother saved me from becoming a she-cowboy. Anyhow, my father insisted on naming me Delma, because it was close to his name, Dale. After Mother died, he became jealous of every man who looked at me. None of them were good enough, but I fell in love with Mark Nelson. True, Mark was a drover, but drovers made ample money if the conditions were favorable. It was a hard life, no life for a married man with his wife left alone for months until the drive was over. On his last drive he went partners with Happy Creele. They hit the market in Wichita at its peak and made a good stake. Happy didn't live to enjoy it. He was killed in a drunken brawl in one of the deadfalls that littered the town. Under their agreement, if anything happened to either of them, the surviving partner would inherit the dead man's share. There was a rumor about Wichita that Mark had his partner killed to get all the money for himself. It was a dirty lie."

Teach shook his head. "Mark wouldn't do a thing like that," he protested.

"Of course not, Red. Mark got out of town before the crowd could get ugly. There was talk of a lynching. He took a roundabout trail out of Kansas through Colorado and Utah before he headed south to Douglas."

"Did he carry the money with him?" Teach asked.

"It was a bank draft. He had little trouble concealing it. When he got back to Douglas, he cashed the bank draft, looked up what relatives he could find of Happy Creele and shared the money Happy would have received with them. He found Happy's folks in Bisbee. Happy's parents were old and the money was a godsend to them. There was also an invalid sister. I loved Mark for his unselfishness and he was determined to give up the trail."

"It looks like this Mexican caper might be his last trail, Delma. He sure is in a hell of a mess right now."

"I know, Red. I am partly responsible for his predicament. That's why I want to go to him. I had no idea his trip across the border could be so devastating."

"Do you reckon your pa made them conditions on purpose, Delma?"

"You mean Pa was hoping he wouldn't come back? I can't believe that, Red. Pa was just testing him. He wanted to see if Mark was a fiddle-foot or if he was ready to settle down. It was Mark's decision to go across the border. He figured that with the money he had made on the drive, he could stock up his range much faster with cheap Mexican cattle. Those Mex longhorns are tough. They've got to be to live down there."

"But Mark already has a ranch," Teach protested.

"A two-room cabin on a hundred acres of land," she pointed out. "To Pa that's no more than a shack. It's in a beautiful spot, I'll agree. Mark planned to build a real house when he got back, and he put down money on a government range lease covering five thousand acres between Apache and Dos Cabesos. That will give him access to open range all the way to the Peloncillo Mountains."

"That's a right fancy dream, Delma. There's many a slip twixt the cup an' the lip, my maw used to say. Right now Mark is on the brink of disaster. Mebbe by now he's tumbled over. Let's hit our blankets. We gotta make an early start. I'll sleep on the other side of the fire. You can take this side. The smoke won't choke you here."

Teach picked up his bedroll and went around the fire, putting the dying embers between them. A coyote howled its mournful cry which was followed by a sharp yapping sound. He looked back at Delma and wondered if the sound frightened her. She still sat by the fire staring into the coals. Teach busied himself rolling out his own blankets and crawling between them, boots and all. He drew his hat across his face to shut out the brilliant stars in the desert sky. He feigned sleep, giving her what privacy she required. He had meant to keep awake until she was settled in her blankets on the other side of the fire, but fatigue defeated him. He drifted into sleep, ignoring the sounds of the night life about him—the skittering, the mewling, the lonely sounds of creatures who adapted themselves to the desert by retreating underground during the hot, dry days and using the cool, still nights in which to gather their food.

After his first deep sleep had worn off, Teach saw that Delma had moved her blankets next to his. He didn't disturb her.

In the first light of morning, Teach awoke to the smell of steaming coffee and sizzling meat. He sat up with a funny feeling. He made no reference to her seeking his side for warmth. It was she who mentioned the incident over their breakfast.

"I hope I didn't disturb you last night, Red," she said.

He hesitated with his answer. It was obvious that an attractive young woman would be disturbing to the man she was lying next to. To deny it might displease her. He chose the subterfuge of a lie. "What do you mean, Delma? I was so plumb tuckered out, I slept like a log."

"I rolled up in my blanket next to you. I was frightened by the night sounds, and I felt safe near you. I slept like a log myself."

"I reckon that makes two logs. We might dream a log cabin between us if we keep that up."

They made good time that day and reached the isolated farm where he had traded horses on his trip north. Rain had been there before them and the ground was still soggy. Teach had a disturbing thought. Could the heavily laden wagons make it without bogging down? It would be days before the caravan would reach there. By that time the ground would have dried out. The Indian woman was alone when they rode into the yard. She came out to meet them.

"*Buenas tardes,* senor." She greeted Teach like an old friend. She looked with suspicion at Delma.

"*Buenas tardes*, senora." Teach returned the greeting. He explained in Spanish that they wished to rest their horses and spend the night.

"Is this your wife, senor?" She indicated Delma.

To avoid a lengthy explanation, he nodded his head and said, "*Si,* senora, this is my wife." He knew it would not be considered proper for Delma to travel with him otherwise.

Delma, who spoke Spanish fluently, gave him a wry smile.

"I'll explain later," Teach told her in English. To the woman he said in Spanish, "Where are the men?"

"You tell them that Santa Barbara is destroyed by the wind, senor. They go there to give help," she told them. "We have much rain here. Put your horses in the stable."

"I'll take care of the horses," he told Delma. He told the woman, "The horse I took from here is coming back with the supply wagons. Is my fine horse still here?"

"The men took the fine horse with them to Santa Barbara. Don Pietro will reward them," she said enigmatically.

Teach doubted he'd ever see the horse again.

"*Gracias*, senora," Delma said. "You are very kind to shelter us."

Teach tended the horses. They ate the beans and tortillas the woman offered, because to bring in their own food would be an insult to her hospitality. Delma praised the tortillas, which were suprisingly tender and tasty.

The woman beamed at her praise. "I meex with the meal some eggs," she explained.

The fresh eggs from the chickens scratching out in the yard made the tortillas more palatable and nourishing. After the meal the woman offered them the bunks the men were not using. Doubtful of the condition of the bunks, Teach demurred.

"I reckon we'll sleep here before the fire, senora. We're used to sleeping on the ground."

The woman shrugged. "Sleep well, then."

Teach and Delma were awakened by the voice of the Indian woman.

After a hearty breakfast of side meat, which the senora proclaimed proudly came from their own pigs, and fresh eggs, Teach and Delma started out.

"We should make Santa Barbara before dark," Teach told her. "If nothing goes wrong, that is."

CHAPTER EIGHT

Mark rose to his feet as he entered the *cantina*. The adobe walls and the intact roof muffled the sound of the wind. It was almost totally dark in the smelly barroom. The pale oval of the bartender's face was visible behind the bar. He stared at Mark as though he were seeing a ghost. Mechanically he put a bottle of tequila on the bar. Against his better judgment, Mark took a drink from the bottle. The fermented cactus juice burned like fire in his stomach, but it did jar him into renewed activity.

"How come, *amigo*, this den of the devil exists without destruction beside the ruined house of God?"

"*Quien sabe*, senor? The church, she protect the *cantina*. The church, she stop the wind and turn it aside," the man explained.

"I've gotta get back to the church," Mark said.

"Why, senor? Pronto we will all be dead," the barkeep warned him.

"We're not dead yet, *amigo*. Only the dead are dead. Save your tequila and mescal. We'll need it for preventing infection."

As Mark prepared to go out and battle the wind, Luis Velasco staggered into the *cantina*. He was bloody from head to foot. His black hair was a snarl on his bare head. Mark looked at him with wonder and a strange respect. A man has many facets to his character. Here was Velasco—a barroom brawler when he was drunk—in this emergency a man of deep pity and valiant effort. Mark shoved the tequila bottle toward him.

"You need a slug of this, Luis. You're about done in. If you don't slow down, you'll be one of the casualties," Mark told him.

Velasco took a long drink from the bottle. He looked blankly at Mark. At first his lips moved but no sound came forth. He took another drink from the bottle and became aware of his surroundings.

"Perhaps the dead are the blessed," he said. "The dead are at peace. They have no more fear, no more pain, no more blind hope. These are my people, senor. To you they are greasers, peons, little more than cattle. But you help them. Why?"

"Because they're human beings, *amigo*, just like me an' you. I've got to get over to the church, Luis. They need help there," Mark said.

"You'll never make it, senor. The devil wind will grab you in his fist and kill you. What good will you do them then?" Velasco warned him.

Mark knew the truth of Velasco's words, but inaction

drove him to the brink of insanity. He felt a sudden urge to drink tequila until his mind felt soggy and oblivion blotted the tragedy from his brain. He couldn't do that. Delma crept into his thoughts. How far away she seemed now—how remote and unattainable. He thought of her warm, brown eyes and the feel of her moist lips on his. There was no way she could know of his terrible condition, of the suffering of these people, and of the heroic efforts of aristocrat and peon alike to lessen their suffering. Perhaps by some miracle, Teach might outrun the storm. He might reach Douglas or Nogales and appeal for help. But help would be too late, too late to do anything but bury the dead and watch the injured in their futile suffering. There was no need to blame anybody but himself for his predicament. His greed for a quick profit and his impatient love for Delma had motivated his trip south of the border. True, the hurricane was an act of God for which he shared no blame. Now he had to find a way out of the trap. At least he was alive—but with his herd of cheap cattle scattered by the storm and his money already spent. His ambitious plan had turned into a fiasco, a fiasco from which he could not escape with conscience and honor until he had done everything possible for these unfortunate people.

His grim thoughts coupled with the stupefying effects of the tequila overcame his physical resistance and he dropped his head on the bar and fell into a sleep of utter exhaustion.

How long he slept he didn't know. When he awakened he noticed an abatement in the wind which was replaced by another, more ominous sound. The barkeep was asleep on the bar, snoring sonorously.

Luis Velasco was gone. Mark gouged the sleep out of his eyes and hawked the bitter taste out of his mouth. A feeling of guilt that he had slept at such a time spurred him into action. He went to the door and looked out. He had no idea what time it was. It was dark outside, but whether from the ominous clouds overhead or the lack of daylight he couldn't tell. He was startled to full consciousness by the slashes of lightning splitting the sky with jagged flame. He was conscious of a sound behind the shuddering rolls of thunder that accompanied the lightning. He stepped out into the splashes of rain and turned his eyes beyond the mine to the hills. The lightning was searing the ground with white flame that brought out in bold relief the wounds and wreckage of the doomed town. Over the hills the heavens were in a black turmoil of congested clouds through which lightning and thunder played a raucous game of ten pins.

It was as though nature was intent upon purging the earth of the destruction she had wrought. The danger to the wind-torn town was evident to Mark. He had seen cloudbursts in the mountains, tons of water catapulted into the upper reaches of the canyons, gaining strength as it grew in volume as it raced toward the narrow mouth. It could move rocks the size of a horse, tumbling them ahead of it until the water reached the open country and spread out, losing its initial force. The water could sweep through the town until it drained off into the dry arroyo that paralleled the main street. There was no defense against it, only escape.

The rain suddenly increased to sheets through which the shafts of lightning were like swords of fire, and the thunder a cacophony of sound like the roaring of a thousand cannons. He tried to see the church, wondering if the remainder of the roof was still intact, but close as it was, the church was invisible. He backed into the *cantina*, the roof of which was leaking under the onslaught of the storm. Cloudbursts spent their energy in short order. He watched the black clouds moving overhead and within a half hour the skies were clear over the mountains. An eerie, translucent light followed in the wake of the storm. He could not tell if it was twilight or dawn. The rain slacked off to a drizzle, and in the eerie light he saw the church still standing. By a quirk of fate the crest of the torrent had been diverted from the town into the arroyo. He saw the reason for it. The mine dump of waste rock extended out into the canyon, and the flood striking it had veered away, leaving only the backwash to cover the street of the town with a foot of water.

As Mark started for the church, he stumbled over something in the swirling water at his feet. He looked down. It was Luis Velasco, his white face turned up to the sky.

Mark had no time to see if Luis were alive or dead. He took hold of the Mexican's long arms and dragged him into the *cantina* out of the water. Then he headed for the church fearful of what he might find there. The gaping hole left by the fallen dome would have funneled the torrential rain into the church, which could become a watery grave for those inside. As he neared the entrance of the church, he was relieved to see that somebody had opened the door and that a shallow stream of water was running out of it. The light was increasing so he deduced that it was dawn. Inside the church he was amazed at what he saw. He had overestimated his own importance. Someone had taken charge and had everything in order. People were crouching or lying on the rough pews, out of the water that ran through the church.

The *padre* was propped up on the side altar at the feet of Saint Joseph. Sister Inez, her shattered wimple replaced by a petticoat draped over her bald head, was praying with and consoling the children and the injured. Mark surmised the petticoat belonged to Lolita, who was passing out communion wafers she had found in a dry box behind the altar. She had also found the barrel of sacrificial wine, which she was doling out sparingly to the men and women who desired it. The able men in the group were sluicing the water running across the floor out through the open door. Lolita spotted Mark and came over.

"Thank God you're safe. Where is Senor Nagle?"

"He's down at the big house." Mark explained what was being done there, and gave unstinted praise to the efforts of the women and even Don Pietro. "Teach took off for the border to bring relief supplies," he explained.

"The gringos helping the greasers, Mark?" she said in mock surprise.

"In a case like this, there are no gringos or greasers, there's just people, *amiga*. You've done more than your share."

"It is nothing. I am a woman," she said simply.

Within an hour the sun came out, hot and bright. It shone upon a havoc of half-wrecked houses, twisted trees, debris scattered the length of the *pueblo*. The water had subsided, draining off into the arroyo. A few people, like zombies, had ventured forth from whatever refuge had saved them and were poking among the ruins like automatons for things of value they had treasured most of their lives. The sun was warm and the ground was steaming. Mark looked up the hill at the mine in the mouth of the canyon expecting to see the people who had taken refuge there emerge from the entrance to the tunnel. There was no activity near the mine. Puzzled, he went on to the *cantina* which still stood in spite of the leaky roof. He found the barkeeper of the *cantina* scooping up water from the puddles caused by the leaky roof. There was no sign of Luis Velasco. Mark inquired about him:

"Where is Velasco, *amigo*? I thought he was dead."

"He was *muerto*, all right. Dead drunk. He finish a bottle of mescal. Then he stagger outside like the loco bull. You fall to sleep, I fall to sleep. I wake up and find Velasco on the floor. I don't know what happen. Everything is meexed up in my head."

"I dragged him in and went to the church. The Sister Inez and Senorita Sanchez have things under control now. I'm going down to the *casa blanco*."

Outside he spied Velasco among the stunned people wandering in the ruins. Velasco had a revolver in his hand. He was prying apart some tangled wreckage. Then he aimed at the wreckage and fired. The grim truth struck home to Mark and sickened him. Velasco was playing God; executing the fatally injured who were still alive. Mark hurried to his side.

"What are you doing, Luis? You killed this man!" Mark exclaimed.

"Look at him, senor. He was no man. His body ees broken. His leg ees cut off. I kill him for mercy. He ees suffering no more. What would you do, senor? Life is hard enough with a whole body. Should I have let him suffer?"

Mark looked away. "I cannot judge you, *amigo*. I grant you killed him out of mercy. I would want the same thing for myself. They kill horses, don't they?"

Then he changed the subject. "I wonder what happened to the people in the mine. None of 'em are comin' out. They should have been safe in the tunnel. I'm goin' up to Don Pietro's house and see how they made out there. You check the mine."

At the big house Mark found the people outside the stable, which was still standing, and Rex Nagle was organizing them into groups.

"Thank God everything didn't go," Mark said fervently. "What we need now is to find what food isn't spoiled."

"That's what I'm doing," Nagle said. "One group is to go through the ruins of the trading post and salvage what food they can find. Others are to go to the granary an' see if the corn is all right. I reckon me an' a couple of *vaqueros* will traipse on down the river an' see if we can rustle up some of them skin-and-bones cattle of your'n."

"First off, before the roundup, why don't you go with a group up to the mine an' see why the people ain't comin' out? Velasco is on his way up there. I'll join you as soon as I check the house," Mark suggested.

"The house ain't in bad shape. Them women, in spite of

their hoity-toity ways, has more guts than most men. A couple of the injured died. We put 'em in the dining room with the cook."

Mark went into the house through the kitchen. He thought about the job ahead of them. The people were hungry. They had to be fed. He would gladly donate some of his cattle, skinny as they were, if they could be found. He stepped around the corpses lying in the dining room and went to the parlor. There he found Magdalena huddled in a corner fast asleep. Senora Oliviera, hollow-eyed, sat on the edge of a chaise longue, her arms still caked with dried blood and the hem of her satin dress ripped off—for use as a bandage, no doubt. Senora Martinos was silently saying her beads. She looked up as Mark entered.

"Is it really over, Senor Mark?" she asked in a dead, tired voice.

"Yes, senora, it's over. Where's Don Pietro?"

"He's looking through the rubble upstairs for a suitable uniform to express his position as the *alcalde*. If he shows pride and courage, it will bolster the people. He had some uniforms in a trunk. They may be dry and imposing enough to serve his purpose."

Don Pietro came in, his short, slightly pudgy body wearing a swallowtail coat and his short legs covered by striped pants. His hair had been neatly brushed back and his beard, though untrimmed, glistened with a touch of pomade. He wore a silk high hat and looked anything but the bedraggled man doing menial chores the day before.

"*Buenas dias*, Senor Mark," Don Pietro said, bowing

slightly. "I shall resume my duties as *alcalde* of Santa Barbara. If you have other matters to attend to, go about them."

"There's enough work for everyone, Don Pietro. People are holed up in the mine and have not come out. I don't know why. Rex Nagle is organizing the people to find food. If we're lucky, we'll find a milk cow about the town. The babies need milk."

"*Si*, senor, this I know. Some of the women are heavy with milk. They must share it. I have here the key to the storehouse. The corn must be rationed," Don Pietro said importantly.

Mark left without extending the conversation. He headed for the mine. On the way he picked up what able-bodied men he could muster. At the entrance to the mine, they saw that the heavy rain and the water, rushing down the side of the hill, had softened the roof of the tunnel and it had caved in. How far back the cave-in extended, it was impossible to see. Exasperated at the never-ending obstructions, Mark turned to the men. "Have any of you hombres worked in this mine?"

"*Si, si.*" Two of the men nodded. "We work the midnight shift, *amigo*. We were not here when the big wind come."

"Do you think you can open up this tunnel?" Mark asked.

"Perhaps, senor, with much work. We need picks and the shovels."

"The picks and shovels are probably all buried or blown away," Mark said.

Another young man spoke up. "We need only the rope,

senor. Up the hill ees one ventilation shaft. With the rope an hombre can climb down into the mine."

Mark, instead of being pleased, was disturbed by the news. The torrential downpour could have flooded the mine and drowned the people inside. Before he could express his fears, he saw a trickle of water seeping from the loose dirt and rock in the tunnel entrance. The trickle became a stream.

"Stand back!" Mark warned them.

They had no sooner cleared the tunnel entrance than the dirt let go and a torrent of water washed the dirt away. As the short-lived flood subsided, he heard voices inside the mine. Before long, the trapped people showed up no worse for the experience. There were women and children among them. They explained how they had climbed into the higher areas and kept above the water. Relieved at the good fortune of the people, Mark designated some of the more able men to form gangs and proceed with the work of cleaning up the town, burying the dead, and searching for food. Then he left to find Nagle. He ran into Luis Velasco, who said he'd been in a small fight. That was why he couldn't come to the mine.

"What you do now, *amigo*?" Luis asked.

"I reckon me an' Nagle is goin' down to the flat an' see if we can round up any of the herd. I ain't very hopeful," Mark said ruefully.

"Amigo," Luis said, "those cattle you buy from Don Jose are not ordinary cattle. Like the peon and the Indian, they have learn to live with the hard life. They seek the chaparral for protection. They lie down in the barranca from the wind. And they eat whatever the earth offers. I

will send some *vaqueros* with you. Me, I find the fine
wagon the women have ride in. It blow away from the
stable, but it no break up. It stop in the chaparral not so
far away."

"*Gracias*, Velasco," Mark said and then continued his
search for Nagle, who also had not been able to get to the
mine. He found him supervising the burial of the corpses
that had been removed from the dining room. He had
already checked out the condition of the town's existing
food supply.

"Let the peons bury their dead. You an' me is goin' to
the river to see if we can scare up some of the cattle," Mark
said.

"We gotta get rid of these bodies afore the blow flies get
to 'em," Nagle explained.

"But we have other things to do. Let 'em bury their own
dead. We gotta saddle up whatever horses we can find and
try to get enough of the cattle to feed the people."

"There's some horses," Nagle told him. "We didn't lose
hardly any."

By the time they were saddled and ready for the
roundup, three of Velasco's *vaqueros* showed up. One of
them was riding a burro; the other two had horses. Mark
led the way toward the river, a grim feeling of defeat
obsessing him. This disastrous delay could mean the loss
of everything he had planned and hoped for. Dale Ford,
Delma's father, would ridicule him, and what Delma
herself would think he was not prepared to consider. This
debacle had not been entirely his fault. He had done the
human thing for the people in the *pueblo*. That was his
only defense. His only satisfaction was that the storm was

over, and that he might gather enough of his herd to make the rest of the drive worthwhile.

As they neared the river, which was still swollen by the rain, his hopes were revived. The pond created by the loop in the river had spread out. The chuck wagon was half-buried in the mud at the edge of the pond. There were cattle grazing on the higher ground on both sides of the river.

CHAPTER NINE

Encouraged by what he saw, Mark was confident his luck had changed. He expressed his feelings to Nagle. "It looks like we might have part of a herd at least, Rex."

"Such as it is," Rex replied without enthusiasm. "It's a far piece to the border, *amigo*. Once there, you might have trouble gettin' these wild Mex cattle across. Mex cattle is suspect."

"There ain't no sign of anthrax, or foot-and-mouth disease among 'em" Mark said defensively.

"I reckon they ain't got strength enough to support the germs," Nagle said with a wry smile.

"As Luis Velasco tole me, these cattle are tougher than whangleather. They can live on cactus an' anchor theirselves against storms," Mark averred.

He called the *vaqueros* over and explained to them in his broken Spanish, "Ride through the chaparral and into the barrancas. Stay this side of the river. Senor Nagle an' me, we'll cross over and pick up what we can find on the other side."

They split up and worked all day, gathering a good percentage of the herd. As the sun went down, Mark examined the half-buried chuck wagon. He found a couple of rifles still on the rack. They had been soaked by the rain that had come through the tattered canvas, but they were now dried out. The rifles were not loaded, but, unlatching the lid of the metal box in which the cook kept perishable food, matches, and ammunition—things that needed to be kept dry—they found boxes of cartridges and six-gun ammunition. There were also beans and flour in the big metal box, and a supply of jerky and hardtack.

"Ain't no sense for us to go back to the *pueblo*, Nagle," Mark opined. "We got a good start on the roundup now. We can make out with hardtack an' jerky. The people in the *pueblo* ain't got any food to spare. If we sleep out, we can get an early start and roust out more of the herd. We can stay here a few days."

"I wonder where the camp cook is," Nagle mused.

"He probably went into town before the wind came up and got drunk with the rest of them." Mark shrugged.

He talked it over with the *vaqueros*, promising them a bonus, and they agreed to the plan. They stayed out several days and had a considerable bunch of cattle spread out on the graze along the river from which the flood water had subsided. One of the *vaqueros* had brought back some cattle to town to help feed the people.

Finally, they all headed for town, taking the rifles and ammunition with them. It was dusk when they had crossed the long mile that separated the river from the town. Not knowing what to expect in the battered town, Mark had his .45 loaded and his gunbelt filled with ammunition. The three *vaqueros*, eager to make up for the mescal they had missed on the search for cattle, rode on ahead of them. As they neared the big house with its growth of shrubs and trees about it, Mark stopped and motioned Nagle over close to him.

"I got an uneasy feelin', Rex," he said in a cautious voice. "There ain't nobody movin' about."

"Yeah, *amigo*, I get what you mean. People should be stirrin' about, lookin' for food or relics in the rubble. Mebbe they're all in the church prayin' for God to fill their bellies," Nagle said, half humorously. "The way I was told, is that God helps those who help theirselves."

"Wait a minute, Rex. Look up the street." Mark pointed to an opening in the trees that gave a view of the street of half-demolished adobe huts. A woman ran from one of the houses and a man ran after her. She was carrying something under her shawl. The man, who wore a strange, wide-brimmed sombrero, took an object away from her. The woman struggled to get the object back. There was an explosion. The woman dropped to the ground. The man kicked her aside and proceeded up the street.

"I'll be damned!" Rex hissed. "Somebody's doin' just like I said—helpin' theirselves."

"Don Pietro said he could control the people in his fine clothes and his silk top hat. I reckon greed or an empty stomach ain't much impressed by fancy duds," Mark said.

The *vaqueros* were riding around the back of the big house. A gun roared and one of the *vaqueros* fell off his horse. The other two slid to the ground and sought sanctuary in the stable.

"I reckon we got vultures amongst us, pardner," Rex averred.

"Get down and take your rifle along, Rex. Somebody must have stumbled on the ruins and decided to help themselves to what booty they can find. If it's Comancheros, God help us. They're worse than the Apache ever was. They're renegades, half-breeds, and even some white men. They'd kill a man for a peso. The women, well, let's not think about the women. There's a lot of silver in the *pueblo*, especially in the church and Don Pietro's house. They could be holding the whole town hostage. If they've drank all the rotgut in the *cantinas*, they'll be in a vicious mood," Mark warned.

"What can the two of us do agin' 'em?" Rex asked.

"I ain't sure, Rex. If we can take over the big house, we can protect the women, if it ain't too late. From the ruins of the upstairs, we'd have a view of the street and we could shoot any suspicious character we see there."

"How we gonna tell if we're shootin' friend or enemy, Mark?"

"I reckon there won't be no town men on the street. The Comancheros wear big hats to keep off the sun. The miners of the *peublo* wear caps to hold their tallow lamps. If they are friends, we can find out at the house. It was no friend who shot that *vaquero*. It was a lookout keeping people away. We got to sneak up on the house, Indian fashion, and if you find a lookout there, try to silence him without firing your gun. If they're holding Don Pietro and the women hostage, they might kill them in reprisal if we start shootin'."

"Have you got a knife, Mark?"

"Just my stock knife. I can slash a man with it, but it would be hard to kill him unless I cut his jugular. Try to get an arm around his neck an' choke him so he can't give a warning. You go around the front, Rex. I'll take the back."

They parted and Mark slithered through the bushes, Indian fashion, dragging his rifle after him. He was disturbed by a nebulous thought. Perhaps the guards were placed outside the house by Don Pietro to prevent anybody from entering the house. He had to take that chance. He had seen two cold-blooded killings and it seemed improbable that they were ordered by Don Pietro. He reached the corner of the house undetected. He sidled around the corner and he could see the rear door of the detached kitchen. The red eye of a quirly glowed in the entrance. He crept forward noiselessly, suspecting the guard's attention was riveted to the stable door through which the two *vaqueros* had disappeared. He was waiting, no doubt, for them to show themselves so he could get a shot at them. Mark picked up a large pebble and threw it at the stable door. The guard leaped to attention and took two steps toward the stable. The man wore a wide-brimmed hat, with a serape draped over his shoulder. His clothing marked him as an invader.

Mark moved noiselessly, his gun at the ready. He

couldn't chance a shot. To hit the man on the head was impossible because of the floppy sombrero. He leaped on the man's back and got his arm about his throat. With his knee in the man's back, he jerked the man's head backward. The man made a gurgling sound. Something snapped and he went limp, his neck broken. Mark eased the limp form to the ground and looked at the evil face frozen in the grimace of death. There was no doubt that the man was a half-breed Comanchero. How many more were there, ravishing the town?

Mark dragged the dead man back and sat him up beside the door so that he appeared to still be on duty. He took the man's gun, his knife, and the belt of ammunition draped across his shoulder. His thoughts turned to what he might find upstairs. Were the women and Don Pietro still alive? He entered the kitchen and found no one there. He hid the bandit's gun and ammo belt where he could get his hands on it if he needed it. He wondered how Nagle was making out. In the dining room he found the cupboards flung open and the valuable silverware and plates and goblets were on the table ready to be carried away. No one was in the dining room, proving that the Comancheros felt quite secure in their sudden raid. How did they know about the stricken town that was ready for looting? There was no time to ponder on the answers; there was only time for action. There was no one in the hall, but he heard a garble of voices coming from the parlor. Cautiously he approached.

He kicked the parlor door open with the heel of his boot and leaped inside, hoping to have the element of surprise on his side. Before he could get his eyes focused, something hit him on the head and he fell just inside the door. When he came to, he was looking up into Magdalena's concerned, beautiful face. Her soft, white hand was rubbing his forehead, and her dark eyes were moist with tears. He forced himself up into a sitting position as the haze in his brain cleared. The room came into focus. The two senoras were seated on the chaise longue, their faces bruised and their dresses torn. Don Pietro lay on the floor, his face bloody. Magdalena's duenna, her dark hair half covering her face, was mouthing curses at the Mexican who dominated the room. He was a man with a large straw sombrero shoved back on his thick, dark hair. His bristly face had the stolid expression of an ox, a face with no trace of humor or humanity in it. A cigarette hung from one lip and he held a rifle across his arm.

"What you do here, hombre?" the man asked.

"Just passin' through, *amigo*. This *pueblo* ain't got much left to offer a man," Mark said. Mentally he was cursing himself for a fool to be caught so easily.

"You a *bandido*, hombre?"

"When it's profitable," Mark lied. "I don't reckon there's much profit here. What are you doin' here, mister? Are you a *policia*?"

"Gringo, I am Escobar Entrada," the man said with pride. "Perhaps you have heard of me?"

Mark had heard of him. He had made a name for himself as a scoundrel, while posing as a supporter of Diaz.

"I've heard of you, Escobar. You are one *bravo*

hombre," Mark said deliberately. "Has Porfirio Diaz given you a license to kill women and children and rob the unfortunate?"

"You talk too much, senor. I could kill you and the rest of these aristocratic swine, but for why? I want only the gold, the silver, and the jewels that are hidden here. Perhaps you can enlighten me as to where they are hidden?"

"And if I tell you where they are, will you leave here without killing us?" Mark asked, playing for time in the hope that Rex Nagle would show up.

"I am not a fool, senor. If you know where are the jewels and the gold, then you must be an *amigo* of the don. If you are a *bandido*, you would have taken the gold and the jewels before now," Escobar said.

Mark realized he was in a precarious position. Killing meant nothing to a Comanchero. He looked at Senora Oliviera. "Let's tell him where the stuff is that he wants, senora. To die for gold is a useless sacrifice," Mark said.

"We have no gold. I spend no money on jewels. There are poor people here, even though the mountain has a heart of silver. The silver is taken to Guadalajara to be smelted down and the money goes to Porfirio Diaz so he can win the allegiance of the army and the aristocrats that Maximilian left behind," the senora said.

"Have you searched the house, Escobar? The top story has been half blown away," Mark suggested.

"My men have search the ruins. They find little. Now they search the town. The miners have stolen the high-grade silver to hide in their homes. My men are now searching there. At the church they find the silver crucifix, and the silver communion plate, the candlesticks, and the chalice."

"How did you learn about the ruined *pueblo* of Santa Barbara, Escobar?"

"We have the *amigos* on the *rancheros*, senor. We are generous with them and they are loyal to us. Those who are not loyal are dead," Escobar said, his swarthy face inscrutable.

At that moment from a darkened corner of the parlor, a shot rang out! Escobar jerked around and raised his gun. Mark saw his chance. He threw himself on the Comanchero's back knocking him to the ground. Mark got his hands around the bandit's throat and squeezed with all the strength in his strong fingers. Escobar struggled to no avail. Suddenly he sagged, all the life gone from his evil body. Mark got up to face Rex Nagle.

"I thought you'd never get here, pardner," Mark said, breathing hard.

"I was lucky to get here at all, pardner. There's two vultures out front and I couldn't see no way to get past them. I came through one of the narrow windows on the side of the house. The wind had blown the glass out," Nagle explained.

"That shot you fired ain't gonna to do us no good. It'll just bring the other vultures runnin'," Mark warned. He picked up the rifle dropped by the man he had choked to death. "Get back from the door. Them buzzards out front will come rushin' in to see what the ruckus is." He motioned to the women to get flat on the floor. No sooner had they complied with his order than the sound of boots came from the hall.

"*Caramba*, Escobar! You no kill the women! We take them with us!" a surly voice growled.

As the men entered the door, Mark killed one and Nagle killed the other.

"You've stirred up a hornet's nest now," Magdalena said.

"It couldn't be helped," Mark told her. "You women go down into the wine cellar and hide behind the casks of wine. Nagle an' me will go up on the second floor. We can hold 'em off from there. It'll be dark in a few more minutes, but the moon is bright. We can see well enough to kill anyone who looks suspicious. Nagle, you go on ahead. I killed the guard at the back door, but I got his rifle and ammo belt. I hid 'em in the kitchen. I'll bring them up with me."

On the top floor, Mark and Nagle lay belly-down in the rubble. On the street of the doomed town there were a couple of Comancheros heading for the one canteen that had escaped destruction. They were evidently intent upon a night of debauchery, unaware that Mark and Nagle were in the town. They had evidently discounted the shots as one of their number killing some peons. Mark killed one of the bandits and Nagle killed the other. It was like shooting clay pigeons in a shooting gallery. After the two shots, things quieted down except for the sounds of shouting and singing at the *cantina*.

"I can't understand," Mark said, "how in hell they knew this town was a disaster area. Escobar, the skunk I choked to death, said that a rancher had told them about the wind and the rain that had destroyed the town. We didn't trail past any ranches close to here. If a rancher helped them, it had to be farther to the north."

"It don't make any difference who told them, they're here. We gotta get rid of them somehow before they go on a drunken spree, killin' everything that moves," Nagle said.

"We can traipse up to the church, or the mine. There must be some local men there," Mark suggested.

"Most of these miners don't carry guns, *amigo*," Nagle reminded him. "Of course, if they're *mucho bravo*, they can use picks an' shovels."

"Against killer guns?" Mark scoffed at the idea.

"Mebbe they've got guns at the church. They could have found some in the town whilst we were roundin' up the cattle."

"Let's go," Mark said. "We ain't doin' no good layin' here."

Downstairs, Mark went below to the wine cellar. There was no light, no sound there. He closed the creaky door behind him and at the same time a wine bottle crashed against the earthen wall beside his head.

"Hold it, *amigos*!" he said aloud. "It's me, Mark Nelson." He struck a lucifer and held it before his face.

"Madre de Dios," Lolita exclaimed, "we could have killed you, Mark."

"Is there a candle here?"

"Si." Magdalena spoke up this time. "We brought candles with us."

Mark struck another lucifer, took a candle, and lit it.

"Are you alone?" Senora Martinos asked.

"Nagle is keeping watch upstairs. It appears the Comancheros are all celebrating at the *cantina*. We are going up to the church. You stay here and be quiet."

"I will go with you, Mark. If you die, I want to die, too," Lolita said.

"What good would that do, Lolita?" Mark rebuked her. "You stay here, go upstairs if you wish, and keep a lookout. You can warn the others if anyone invades the house."

"You mean she can warn us of our death or capture. For me it would be death of my own doing rather than be a captive of those animals," Magdalena said scornfully.

"Don't kill yourself too soon, Magdalena. I'm goin' to the mine an' get some blasting powder. We might blow up the *cantina* and all the scum inside," Mark told her.

"You don't know where the blasting powder is stored in the mine. By the time you find it, everything will be over," Senora Martinos said stoically.

"I'm sure to find some miners in the church. One of them can go with me. How is Don Pietro?" he inquired.

Senora Oliviera's voice came from the shadows. "He is still alive but senseless from the blow on the head. We managed to get him down here. The rest is in the hands of God."

Mark left them in their somber hideout. His mind was a dismal fog of unsavory thoughts. Magdalena's threat of suicide rather than surrender haunted him. The reason for her threat depressed him. Comancheros ravished and degraded women. And sometimes they were shot as so much excess baggage. Whatever happened this night, it must not come to that. Lolita, who was on his heels as he emerged from the cellar, might be a match for the pigs, but not a protected girl like Magdalena.

CHAPTER TEN

When they reached Nagle, who was waiting for Mark, Mark turned to Lolita. "Can you shoot a gun, Lolita?" he asked her.

"*Si, si, amigo*. I am one good straight-shooter. I can kill a jackrabbit at one hundred meters."

"Good, Lolita. Take this rifle and go to the upstairs floor. If you see any of the *bandidos* with the big hats coming this way, shoot 'em," Mark instructed her. He gave her the rifle he had taken from the guard out back.

"Maybe I not see you some more, Mark. I am your woman. You fight for me in the *cantina* in Nocariza. Embrace me for the last time, *amigo*," she said in a shaky voice.

Mark, touched by her sincerity, put his arms about her and held her close.

"This won't be our last meeting, Lolita. No matter what happens, I'll get you out of this. Don't kill yourself needlessly. If you're captured, I'll rescue you one way or another. Remember that."

"I no kill myself, *amigo*. I will kill the dogs who touch me," she assured him.

Taking plenty of ammunition, Mark and Rex took a surreptitious route to the church. They passed behind the *cantina*, which was a cacophony of laughter, curses, and ribald singing. A man was smoking outside. He caught sight of Mark and Nagle before they spotted him.

"Where you go, *amigo*? You still look for valuables? There is little left in this *pueblo*," the man said in Spanish. "Come to the *cantina*. We have the *fiesta*. We have some senoritas inside. Soon we drink all of the mescal, tequila, and the cerveza." The man laughed drunkenly.

Nagle, whose Spanish was better than Mark's, spoke up. "We go to the church for one more look around, *amigo*."

"You loco. We take already the tabernacle, the chalice, the candlesticks, everything. Ramon Basta with two men are looking for valuables at the *casa grande*. You come from there?"

"No," Nagle lied. "We look in the ruins of the shops down the street. We find some silver and tooled leather stuff."

"I no see you too good, *amigos*. How are you called?"

Mark tensed. To give false names would give them

away, and they knew none of the names of the Comancheros.

"We will come closer to give you a good look," Mark said.

"I no understand your voice, hombre," the man said suspiciously.

Mark walked boldy up to the Comanchero, his gun concealed behind him. The brim of his tall hat shaded his face from the moonlight. The Comanchero's hat did the same. Mark knew a gunshot would bring all hell down upon them, but he couldn't knock the bandit out as long as he wore his sombrero. The man was scowling at Mark and Nagle, unsure of himself. Boldly Mark knocked the man's sombrero off his head and at the same time he brought his gun down on the black tousled hair with killing force. The man fell without a sound. Mark retreated back toward Nagle, who was keeping watch. At the same time a man came out of the *cantina* calling a name. Mark motioned Nagle to crouch down in the bushes. The newcomer began searching among the bushes.

"What's the matter, Fernando, are you drunk?" the man said as he stumbled over the prostrate form of the dead man. He turned the body over and struck a match. He let out a curse in Spanish. "You got blood all over your head, Fernando. *Madre de Dios*, you are *muerto*, dead!" The man started running toward the *cantina*.

Nagle raised his gun to take a shot at the man. Mark pulled his arm down.

"Let him go. The half-drunk buzzards will come

rushing out of the *cantina*. Sneak up close and we'll kill 'em as they come out," Mark suggested. "We can't barge into the place and start shooting. They've got some *muchachas* in there with 'em. They could be killed."

Creeping quickly through the brush, they reached a point across from the door of the *cantina*. The men came straggling out, unaware of their danger. Mark and Nagle opened fire at the same time. They downed the first two men before the others comprehended what was happening. They killed two more. The men inside the *cantina*, eager to see what was going on, pushed those ahead of them into the open. Mark signaled to Nagle and they changed positions, angling around to the front of the *cantina*.

Then Mark and Nagle killed the men as they emerged. Mark heard a sound behind him. He whirled around and saw two bandits who were rummaging in the ruins of the other *cantina*—the wrecked one across the street— looking for bottles of booze that had not been broken. One of the men raised his gun. Mark dropped as a bullet whistled past his head. He and Nagle were caught in a crossfire.

"Take the front, Rex! I'll get those other buzzards!"

Before he could get a bead on the shadowy forms in the ruined *cantina*, another bullet hit him in the hip, spinning him to the ground. Thank God, they're drunk, he thought as he fell. Otherwise he would have been dead. He cursed himself for having fallen into the trap. His gun had slipped from his hand as he fell and he groped for it, waiting for the next shot to smash him into oblivion. He got to his knees. He heard a shot close to him, but it didn't strike him. He looked around. In the bright moonlight he saw three figures coming from the direction of the *casa grande*. More bandits, he thought.

Then he realized they weren't shooting at him. He got hold of his gun and killed a man with a rifle who was emerging from the ruined *cantina*. Soon the shooting stopped. Everything was quiet.

He heard a voice shouting at him. He was dreaming—he had to be dreaming. It was a girl's voice. It was Delma Ford's voice! Her arms were around him, her soft lips were searching for his lips. He relished the contact, afraid to speak for fear the dream would fade. It didn't fade. It spoke in a fervent voice.

"Thank God, we got here in time, honey. We've been riding since sunup hoping to get here by tonight," the voice said.

"What's this all about?" Mark asked in a dazed voice. He saw Teach standing there beside Lolita.

"When we got here, we stopped at the *casa grande* and were almost shot by Lolita here, who was guarding the place. I yelled at her and she recognized my voice. She told us about the Comancheros raiding the place, and about you and Rex going in search of help. I came to find you and they insisted on coming along. Delma had her own gun and Lolita had the rifle you had left with her."

"You got here just in time," Nagle said. "We was bracketed by their guns."

"Were you hit?"

"I got a slug that grazed my hip and knocked me down," Mark admitted.

"I'd better look at it," Delma said.

"I'd rather look at you, honey. You got some explainin' to do."

"Later. It's one long story. It can wait."

Mark stood up. His hip stung, but held him. "We gotta look in the *cantina* and see if there's any more of the buzzards in there."

They found two girls and an older man.

"Are you all right?" Mark asked the girls.

"Si, si, senor. We are all right."

Teach, by Mark's side, exclaimed, "This hombre is one of the men from the isolated rancho we stopped at. I told him about the trouble here and I left Don Pietro's thoroughbred with him in exchange for a fresh mount on my way north."

Mark turned to the whiskered Mexican. "Did you lead the Comancheros here, hombre?" he asked grimly.

"They make me and my *compadre* show them the *pueblo*. They take the fine *caballo*. My *compadre* try for run away. They kill him," the man said.

"I'm goin' up to the church to see if everything is all right there," Mark said.

"I'm going with you, honey. I'm not leaving you out of my sight again."

"It's a miracle that you're here, Del," Mark said.

"You and Delma go to the big house and explain things to them," Teach said. "Me an' Nagle will search the church and the mine. There ain't no sense exposing the girls to possible danger. Delma can tell you what happened in Douglas."

Mark agreed with feigned reluctance. He wanted to be with Delma, still unable to believe that she was actually there. He could still feel the pressure of her moist red lips on his. Lolita accompanied Mark and Delma down the street of ruined businesses and homes. Lolita was thoughtful. Delma clung to Mark's arm. Lolita broke the silence.

"Your fiancee ees very pretty, Mark," she said gravely. "Tell me one thing, *amigo*, are her kisses better than mine?"

"She ain't gonna be my fiancee for long, Lolita. I mean to marry her as soon as possible. I'll kiss her again right now, an' let you know who's ahead," he chuckled.

"What's this all about, Mark. Did you kiss all the senoritas in Mexico?" Delma needled him.

"Only the deservin' ones," Mark said with a grin.

"All right, kiss me, you Lothario, and let me know how I stack up," Delma demanded.

Mark turned sober eyes on her. "If you had been in the church during the awful storm, and watched Lolita helping the women and the children until she was exhausted, you would have kissed her yourself, honey."

"I'm sorry," Delma apologized. "I didn't mean to be catty. I saw the destruction at the big house, and I can see the damage here. It must have been awful."

"There's no words to describe it, Del. It was pure hell." He went on to tell her of the collapse of the dome and the buried priest. He told her about the trouble at the big house and how he and Nagle had managed to kill the bandits who held the women hostage. Then he answered Lolita's plaintive question.

"When I kissed you, Lolita, I meant it, but in a different way. You deserve more than a random kiss. For what you did an earthly reward would be shoddy. I reckon you'll be rewarded properly in heaven."

"I doubt I will go to heaven." Lolita said frankly. "*Purgatorio*, maybe. I am content to be rewarded on earth, *amigo mio*."

At the big house, Mark brought the fugitives up from the wine cellar. Don Pietro had regained consciousness and was as alert and officious as ever. When they had settled down, Delma told them what had happened in Douglas.

"The people chipped in like true neighbors. It didn't matter that the town of Santa Barbara was a town of Mexicans and Indians. My father sent along a wagon full of supplies and medicine. He also sent along some cowboys to guard the supplies and help get Mark's cattle home. Even Doby Evers is sending along a Conestoga full of food and what clothing could be collected from the women of the town."

"I reckon he's also sending some of his men, eh?" Mark interrupted.

"Of course. A wagon load of food and clothing would be raided by the Yaquis before it got five miles below the border," Delma reminded him.

"They could also interfere with the trail drive and delay me or prevent me from getting the cattle on my range in time," Mark said grimly. "If I don't get a reasonable herd of cattle on the grass before the deadline, my government lease will expire and the range will be open to the first man who can stock it."

Delma's brown eyes gave him a level look, and she ran her tongue across her full lips. "We'll have to prevent him from delaying us, honey," she said seriously. She added, "Besides, Doby Evers has his eye on your lease."

"What do you mean by *we*? It's not your problem, Del."

"Oh, but it is. Your problems are my problems from now on, Mark. That is, unless you prefer these beautiful senoritas below the border." She turned her eyes on Magdalena, who, disheveled as she was, looked every inch a lady.

"Muchacha," Senora Martinos said to Delma, "you, too, are beautiful, but it is a strong beauty with purpose and loyalty behind it."

"That's right, Mama," Magdalena said with a mirthless smile, "I am to be educated and groomed to be an asset to some smirking nabob left over from the days of Maximilian. I have no need for purpose and loyalty, only for obedience. I cannot have Mark, the man I love."

"You shall have no loves while I exist, *muchacha*." Magdalena's duenna spoke up from the background.

"I reckon I got something to say about this!" Mark silenced them. He took Delma in his arms and kissed her warmly in front of them. "I made a mistake coming down here to buy cheap cattle so I could win you like a lottery prize. I should have taken you to Tucson and married you in spite of your pa."

Delma looked up and gave him eye for eye. "What's stopping you, *amigo*? There's still time. Pa can't interfere with us here."

"What do you mean?"

"You said the *padre* at the church didn't die. He might still have the strength to perform a wedding ceremony," she said defiantly.

Mark felt a surge of feeling at her words—mixed feelings. Love for her was ignited by the simple truth of her suggestion. Marry her here and travel back to Arizona as man and wife. Discretion dampened his ardor. There were many dangers between here and Arizona. As he had been warned, they were on the *Pista del Muerto*, the trail of death.

What other travails lay ahead? He didn't want Delma to reach Arizona a widow, or worse still the wife of a cripple. Her willingness to accept those dangers made his love for her even greater—but he would not risk them.

"I love you, Del, and your suggestion is an offer hard to resist. But I made a deal with your pa, and I can't break it behind his back. When we get married, everything has to be aboveboard. Your pa would never let you live down the fact that you acted behind his back. He would make sure I never had a proper ranch and you would come to resent his actions. You're his world, and in his own stubborn way he loves you very much. He made the conditions of our marriage as tough as he dared, hoping I would *not* succeed. Then he could keep you to himself a while longer."

She pushed him away from her. "I don't think you know just what you're saying, Mark. Teach will marry me. Remember, we traveled three days together. We got along very well. Teach is not a *manana* man. He accepts today and lets tomorrow take care of itself."

"I reckon tomorrows never come, sweetheart, they just

merge into today and the mistakes of today could become tomorrow's nightmare. The town's littered with dead Comancheros who were bent on looting and killing. All their tomorrows are lying out there with them," Mark said.

Don Pietro spoke up. "You are a wise man, a brave man, *amigo*. We shall erect a monument for you in the plaza once the town is rebuilt. For us isolated greasers, you have risked death, imperiled your fortunes, delayed your future. A woman who gets you for a husband can be sure you are not a man of impulse, anger or thoughtlessness."

"Don Pietro makes me feel ashamed of myself, honey," Delma said, putting her arms about him. Mark caressed her soft, brown hair.

"You are free to go, Senor Mark. I will take over the town. The able-bodied men can bury or burn the dead. The women can nurse the crippled. Whatever cattle you find by the river or in the foothills, take with you with our blessing."

"*Gracias*, Don Pietro," Mark said. "The supply wagons will be here in a few days. In the meantime, me an' my buddies will continue to round up what cattle we can. What happened to Luis Velasco. Do you know?"

"No, senor. He did not come to the *casa*," Don Pietro said.

"Well, I figure he'll turn up," Mark said. "It's safe to sleep the rest of the night. We'll all need our strength in the morning."

Before they settled down for the night, Teach and Nagle came down from the church and the mine.

"They didn't need us up there, Mark," Teach explained. "Most of the injured have been moved to the church school, which was protected by the mine dump which turned the water away from it. The able women are takin' care of the ones who are laid up. The *padre* is able to sit up but he's in a daze. He keeps mumblin' prayers to Saint Joan, or somebody, to perform a miracle and restore the town. The men are searching the mine for shovels and picks to help Saint Joan with her miracle."

In the morning they ate what food they could find in the wrecked kitchen and took some scraps along to sustain them for a day or two. Mark told Teach and Nagle, "We'll search the river and the foothills for what additional stock has survived the storm. By the time help gets here from Douglas, we might have enough stock to make the drive worthwhile. We'll get Luis Velasco to help us. He knows the country."

A voice spoke from the dining-room door. "You're not going without me, Mr. Nelson." Delma was standing there ready for the roundup.

"It ain't goin' to be no picnic, honey," Mark said soberly.

"I've never asked for a picnic, Mr. Nelson. You can't stop me from helping out. We're partners from now on, remember?"

Mark knew the futility of argument. They went out to the barn to see about horses. Mark was in the lead. As he stepped through the door of the stable, his voice exploded in a fervent curse. Just inside the door lay the body of Luis Velasco. His throat had been cut from ear to ear. Blood formed a red halo about his dark head!

CHAPTER ELEVEN

On seeing Velasco lying dead in a pool of blood, Mark's mind convulsed in a confusion of thoughts. Were there still some Comancheros alive in the town? He recalled the one he had killed near the kitchen door. Could that man have come back to life? Then he also remembered the *vaqueros* who had escaped into the stable after their partner had been killed. One of them could have attacked Luis as he entered the barn and cut his throat thinking he was the Comanchero who had surprised them. Conjecture was useless. Velasco was dead and had to be accounted for to Don Jose Martinos.

"What the hell's goin' on here, Mark?" Teach demanded looking over Mark's shoulder.

Mark stepped over Velasco's body. "Somebody cut

Velasco's throat," he said in a tight voice.

"Well, I'll be damned!" Nagle said, looking at the body in the pale light of morning. "I figured Luis as the last one to die. The man was so full of energy and contrary emotions. His *vaqueros* will be hard to handle without him to threaten and cajole them."

"You're right, there, Nagle," Mark agreed. "Luis was loyal to Don Jose, but these riffraff *vaqueros* ain't loyal to nobody. They could take off and solicit some help from the Yaquis and come back to steal the whole herd."

"We'll worry about that later. First, let's get on with the roundup. The miners will find Velasco's body and bury it along with the others," Teach suggested.

Delma, clinging to Teach's arm, took one look at Velasco and said, "I think I'll stay here and help the women. You men can go after the cattle."

Reluctantly, Mark agreed with Teach, though he felt he owed Luis more than that. He recalled Velasco's valiant efforts to help the people of the town, and his execution of the hopelessly crippled man trapped and dismembered in the ruins. That was part of life; now Luis Velasco had joined that brotherhood of equality in which there is no title, no wealth, no suffering but the calm acceptance of the final assignation. He was relieved that Delma had decided to stay behind.

Down by the river they stoppped at the chuck wagon. Most of the water had drained away from it. They found the cook's body some distance away, buried in the slimy mud. Tying their ropes to the wagon, they managed to pull it free of the silt and water with the combined efforts of their horses. They didn't bother cleaning it out. Their chief concern was to gather as many cattle as they could before the supply wagons arrived. The sun came out hot and bright. One result of the rain was a fresh growth of grass and shrubbery. The cattle near the river that had been gathered previously were still contentedly grazing among the trees and the bunches of chaparral. The three of them split up and headed for the foothills. By nightfall they had added more than a thousand head to the cattle grazing along the river. They met at the chuck wagon, tired but pleased with the results of their efforts.

Mark suggested they camp out for the night and get an early start in the morning. "I reckon the *pueblo* ain't goin' to be a rose garden with the hot sun burnin' down on the death and destruction," he opined.

They agreed and built a fire in the grove of cottonwoods along the river. Soon the smell of boiling coffee which, among other things they had found in the wrecked kitchen, filled the air, and the sizzle of side meat and eggs added to the aroma.

Enjoying an after-dinner quirly built from Bull Durham Teach had brought from Douglas, Mark remarked, "I'm a mite worried about the rest of the drive without Luis Velasco to ramrod his men. Luis was loyal to Don Jose, and he had vowed to protect the women with his life. I reckon he's given up his life, and not for the women but for the compassion he felt for his countrymen visited by disaster."

"Surely we'll get some help from the men who are protectin' the relief supplies," Teach hazarded. "Delma's pa is sendin' some good men down along with the supplies."

"So, no doubt, is Doby Evers," Mark reminded him. "I don't figger Evers's men have orders to break their necks protectin' my interests."

"We ain't gonna solve none of them problems until they show up," Nagle opined. "If Doby's cavvy aim to start trouble, they'll lay low until we reach the border."

"In the meantime," Mark said ruefully, "they can delay my drive by various means, so that I'll lose my lease on the Culebra Range."

"So what?" Teach asked. "There's other range to be had, *amigo*."

"Not as good as the Culebra, an' not borderin' on my present ranch," Mark reminded him.

"There ain't no sense in arguin' about a future as shaky as ours," Nagle said, yawning. "I reckon I'm goin to hit the sack."

In the morning they started out after an ample breakfast. By nightfall, in addition to the cattle that drifted to the river of their own accord for water, they had a sizable herd ready to be shaped into a trail herd. They had run across some dead cattle that had succumbed to the storm, but not as many as Mark had expected. As they neared the chuck wagon at sundown, they saw two separate clouds of dust heading for Santa Barbara.

"Them must be the supply wagons," Teach remarked.

"Thank God they made it," Mark said fervently. "And much earlier than we thought. I reckon we might as well head for town an' give 'em a hand in unloadin'."

When they reached the town they found that most of the dead had been buried in the deep trenches gouged into the arroyo by the flood, and covered over with rocks and debris. The smell of death still lingered in the warm air. The wagons had arrived and Don Pietro was taking charge of the storing of the supplies in whatever shelter was still available. Much of the food was stored in the wine cellar of his house, where it could be protected against pillage. The peons were unloading the wagons which gave the men who had brought them a chance to sample Don Pietro's imported port or what tequila or mescal could be salvaged from the ruins.

Mark talked with Dale Ford's men. "You hombres made good time, Jock," he said to Jock Miller, who was in charge of the freight wagon.

A voice spoke up from the other side of the big wagon. "Ah reckon we was almost attackeded by some Yaquis, but ah scahed them off." The speaker, a gangling black man, came around the wagon.

"Why, Joshua Grant, how come you're on this expedition?" Mark greeted him.

"At the last minnit Mistah Ford, he figured I'd come in handy iffen the Mex or the Indians caused us any trouble. The greasers an' the Indians don't rightly understand me, but I'm more their color, so them who ain't afraid of me figure I'm more to be trusted than a gringo."

"If there was only one wagon in our cavvy, they might have chanced it. Two wagons with outriders was too chancy for 'em to tackle," Jock opined.

Mark called over to Clay Walters, who was ramrodding Doby Evers's men and his Conestoga with supplies. "If your men want to help me get my herd on the trail, I'll pay 'em extra for their trouble when we get to Douglas."

Clay Walters had deceptively genial features with a

shock of unruly blond hair escaping from under the brim of his black sombrero.

"You mean *if* you get to Douglas. Do you know what the Mex call this trail you're takin'?"

"Yes. How could I forget it? *Pista del Muerto*—the trail of death. Lolita keeps reminding me of it," Mark said.

"Who's Lolita? She sounds interestin'," Clay Walters said.

"She's a girl with the compassion of a saint and the courage of a tigress. Right now she's up at the school behind the church. The school was saved by the protection of the mine dump. She can sing like a bird, and shoot as well as Annie Oakley."

"In case you got notions, Walters, she's my girl," Teach said flatly.

"Is that so? Mebbe you ain't had a right kind of competition, Teach. Might be she'd prefer something better than an owlhooter," Clay said with a mirthless grin.

Mark stepped in to end the exchange of words before it developed into a fight. Teach had a temper and Walters was deliberately trying to goad him.

"We ain't gonna be here long enough to find out her preference. Talk to your men, Walters. Those who want to help work my herd must show up at the stables at first light. We'll take enough of these supplies to see us to the border."

Just then Delma came out with the other women to watch the unloading. She still wore her range outfit, but her tanned face had been scrubbed to a healthy glow, and her light brown hair was parted in the middle and fell on either side of her youthful face. Magdalena stood close beside her. The contrast between the two girls was obvious. Delma was a real Western girl, strong and erect, her brown eyes flinching at nothing. Yet she was soft, too, soft and yielding when the occasion called for it. Magdalena on the other hand was tall and calm, her oval face, with its blue eyes and red lips, radiating self-assurance. The air of mystery behind her eyes added to the picture. She was an aristocrat but not to the point of being useless.

"We've come to give you a hand, senor," she said to Joshua Grant.

"Ah'd 'preciate holdin' your hand, senorita," Josh said with an attempt at humor, "but this ain't no kind of work for a 'ristocratic lady."

"We're women first, Mr. Black Man, and aristocrats when the situation calls for it," Senora Oliviera rebuked him. "Soon it will be dark. The people will need some of this food tonight, and we women will have to pass it out. We've been on skimpy rations for the last few days."

As they worked they talked about the wind and the flood and the bloody invasion of the Comancheros. Mark drew Magdalena aside. "What about the wagon for you women?"

"Don Pietro has had it cleaned and the wheels greased," she told him. "Our driver survived and our horses came back to the stable. There's only one uncertain thing. Without the protection of Luis Velasco, we will have to rely on you to keep the *vaqueros* in line. They were loyal to Luis, but with him gone they'll be loyal only to themselves."

"It was too bad about Luis, Magdalena. I came to

understand him pretty well during the crisis. With the help of the men Dale Ford sent down with the wagons, we can keep the *vaqueros* in line."

Delma came over to them. "What are you two conniving about?" she asked with a smile. "I'm the *segundo* from now on, Mr. Nelson."

"We ain't connivin'," Mark said, "we're just makin' arrangements. You, my sweet, will ride with the ladies in their wagon."

"We've been on roundups together before, Mark. Did you ever see me shirk my job?" she asked him.

"Look, Miss Boots an' Spurs, you ain't no child no more to be pampered and tolerated. You might get used to takin' orders an' forget your pa treated you like a *son*. When we're married you'll stay home an' mind the kids an' keep house," he warned her.

"Me be good squaw," she quipped, "me take papoose on back, me cook on chuck wagon. Me no trust you with young petticoats running loose on range."

"You can trust him, Delma," Magdalena said. "Take my word for it. He's a one-woman man and you're the woman. He's making this crazy trail drive to prove his devotion."

"Looky here, you chicks, we got two more uncertain weeks on the trail. Don't complicate things with petty bickering. You women ride together. Dave and I will keep an eye on your wagon. Clay Walters will keep Evers's men in line."

"Who'll keep Clay Walters in line? He's quite a lady's man," Delma said.

"I'll personally keep Clay Walters in line, honey."

"It will be crowded in the wagon," Magdalena reminded him. "Lolita will be coming along."

"That's all right," Delma told her. "You, your mother, and your duenna can sleep in the wagon. Lolita and I will bed down under it. I prefer the stars and fresh air."

The next morning was spent lining out the herd. Mark felt lucky to have as many cattle left as he had. He estimated there were three thousand head, which meant that he had lost a quarter of his original four thousand. If he made it to the border with what he had he would be lucky. He wasn't complaisant about the prospects. The closer they came to the border, the more chance there was of running into renegade Indians, criminals on the dodge from the law, or *bandidos* over which the government of Diaz in Mexico City had little control.

Clay Walters and Doby Evers's other three men agreed to join up with Mark and all the Ford men, including their foreman, Jock Miller. That made two men to drive the nearly empty wagons, and about a half dozen new hands to help handle the herd. The three remaining *vaqueros* left of Velasco's personal company were in the cavvy, but Mark was loath to trust them. They were quiet, surly men but competent in the handling of cattle. Part of their silence could be attributed to Luis Velasco's death. They were loyal men, eager to follow a strong, courageous leader. Bereft of their leader they were like children separated from their parents. Mark took a positive attitude toward them, giving orders in a firm but quiet way so as not to arouse their resentment. Just as he mistrusted them, they, in turn, mistrusted any gringo.

The herd of half-wild, lean cattle settled down to the routine of the trail. The grass, watered by the timely arrival of thunder showers, was better than he had hoped for. They followed the trail between the Yaqui River and the foothills of the Sierra Madre Occidentals, which would take them through more rugged country before they reached Agua Prieta just south of Douglas. If the Indians were going to give them trouble, it would be in that rugged country.

Mark called Teach to his side. "Take the point for a spell, Dave. I want to check on the women. There seems to be a commotion going on there."

"What d'you mean, commotion?" Teach asked, shading his eyes and looking ahead at the wagon.

"For one thing, it appears there ain't nobody drivin' the horses. Them nags is slowin' up an' followin' the best grass. If they fall behind us, they'll be eatin' our dust for the rest of the day," Mark said.

"Don't get too cozy with them three fillies, Mark. Delma's yours if you reach your range in time, an' I call Lolita mine to keep her happy, but I ain't the marryin' type. I ain't sure that Magdalena is happy with her lot. She's got a hanker for you, I know that. Them gals is as different as day, night, an' August."

"Are you tryin to riddle me, Dave? Them gals is just a responsibility I aim to discharge, even though I was finagled by a fickle fate into looking after 'em. I defended Lolita at the risk of my neck and any woman feels for a *bravo* hombre who is fool enough to fight for her. Magdalena has lost the protection of Luis Velasco, so I have to take over. She ain't got no real hanker for me. She just has an aversion to bein' penned up in a convent. And finally, never in God's world did I expect Delma to show up down here."

"Amen," Teach intoned. "That's the way life is, pardner. It's the unexpected that makes it interestin'. It's like a poker game with deuces wild; you don't know what might turn up. You keep playin' the fool game even though you know that the Big Dealer up in the sky allus takes the final pot."

"Save your platitudes for church, *amigo*, if you ever get inside one. The women ain't responsible for the fix we're in. I aim to see they arrive across the border safe, but in the meantime there ain't no place for romance."

Mark rode on ahead, curious and a little incensed by the erratic driving of the women's wagon. The older man assigned by Velasco to drive the wagon had seemed responsible up to now. Mark rode directly to the front of the wagon and found the reins dragging on the ground. The horses, freed of control, were browsing on the grass and tender shoots of greasewood. Mark stiffened in the saddle as he saw the driver lying on the seat, apparently asleep.

"Wake up, *amigo*!" he shouted at the driver. "Wake up!" The man made no movement.

Mark rode to the head of the team and stopped them. He picked up the trailing reins and wound them about the brake handle. He shouted at the man again, louder this time. He stood up in the stirrups for a better look at the driver, angered by the thought that the man was drunk. He heard voices behind him. He looked around at Delma and Lolita, who had come out of the wagon to see what the commotion was all about.

"Is anything wrong, honey?" Delma asked.

"Your driver is dead drunk. Didn't you feel the wagon meandering?"

"No. I was reading and Dona Estrella was knitting. Lolita and Magdalena were playing cards. Anything to pass the time. The driver must have cached a bottle of mescal under the front seat," Delma hazarded.

"I don't think so," Lolita said. "He never drink before we come to Santa Barbara."

"What happened there would drive any man to drink," Mark said. He climbed up on the front wheel and took hold of the driver's arm. He repeated, "Wake up!" To Delma, he said, "Where are the other wagons?"

For answer the man rolled off the seat onto the footboard.

"He's not asleep, he's dead," Delma said urgently. "Dona Estrella gave them permission to hurry along and let the people in Douglas know how things are," she added.

"He's dead, all right," Mark agreed. "Help me get him down on the ground so I can examine him. I didn't hear any gunshot."

They slid the driver's body over the front wheel and lay it on the ground. Mark searched for a wound, but there was none.

"There's a jug in the corner under the seat," Delma said. She climbed up and brought the jug down. She uncorked it and held it to her nose. "This mescal don't smell right," she announced, wrinkling her nose. She held the jug out to Mark. "Do you think the drivers of the wagons that pulled out drank some of it?"

Mark smelled the jug and took a taste of the contents. "This liquor has been polluted with arsenic—enough to kill a horse. Whoever sold it to him deliberately meant to kill him. The arsenic doesn't work at once. He's been pulling on that jug for the last few days. It finally caught up to him."

While they were talking the herd was passing them by. The dust, the noise, and the smell of the cattle pervaded the air. The drovers looked over at them with unabashed curiosity. Out of the cloud of dust, rode Clay Walters, Doby Evers's ramrod. Clay pushed his warped Stetson back on his shaggy blond hair and sleeved the sweat off his forehead. He dismounted and spoke to the girls with his engaging smile.

"What's the matter here, *muchachas*? Did your driver get drunk on you?"

"Ask the boss," Delma said sharply, indicating Mark Nelson.

"I didn't figure him as boss of the women. You gals have been doin' all right without him to wet nurse you," Walters said, his smile unchanging.

Mark stepped in front of Walters. "This ain't no time for wisecracks, Clay. This man's been murdered."

"Murdered? I didn't hear no gunshot, Nelson."

"There's more than one way to kill a man, Walters. You can face him with a gun, knife him in the back, or play the rattler an' poison him."

"Wait a minute, Nelson. Why are you addressin' your

remarks to me? I ain't one to gun down an old man; I ain't no back stabber, an' I ain't no rattlesnake."

"Somebody plotted the old man's death," Mark insisted.

"Why suspect me?" Walters said in a deceptively soft voice.

"Because Doby Evers, your boss, has declared openly that he intends to take over my lease on the Culebra Range."

"How could killin' this old driver hold you back?"

"It could be a warnin', Walters. This driver is only the first one to die. There can be others."

"What others, the women?"

"Yeah, mebbe the women, Clay."

"Who would want to kill these purty ladies?" Walters said, eyeing Delma.

Mark hesitated before replying. Who would want to kill the women? The three *vaqueros* who were in the crew without the restraint of Luis Velasco to discipline them might get ideas of their own. They were smart enough to know of the ransom to be collected for the release of a person of importance. Don Jose would pay any price to insure the lives and safety of his wife and daughter. Once they were released he would deal with the kidnappers if he had to turn all Mexico upside down to find and execute them. Mark knew the fallacy of his reasoning even as he constructed it. The unschooled *vaqueros* had neither the knowledge nor the means to fabricate an ingenious plot. As Mark groped for answers, Dona Estrella and Magdalena came out of the wagon and joined them.

CHAPTER TWELVE

"What's the difficulty here, Mark?" Magdalena asked.

Mark explained what had happened. Dona Estrella smelled the jug that still contained some of the mescal.

"Are you sure the mescal killed him? This mescal smells of the poison we use at home to kill rats. Pablo, the driver, was no fool. If there had been enough of the poison in the jug to kill him, he would have tasted it. He's an old man. He could have died of other causes—heart failure, for instance, or a seizure of the brain."

Jock Miller, foreman on Dale Ford's crew, came back from the herd, which, by now, was some distance ahead of the women's wagon.

"What's goin' on here?" Jock inquired. "You women is

supposed to keep ahead of the drive to escape the smell and the dust."

Mark explained what had happened and added, "Senora Martinos doubts that the arsenic killed the driver."

"What sense does it make to kill the driver? Do you think somebody hoped to get at the women?" Miller asked.

"In broad daylight?" Magdalena countered. "There's five of us women. It would take five good men to subdue us. None of us are weaklings and the jungle hasn't been entirely bred out of us. I suggest we bury Pablo here, and get a new driver."

"We don't need a new driver," Delma said firmly. "I'll drive the wagon."

Mark put an arm around her shoulders. "I'm afraid that won't do, honey. A wagon load of unprotected females would prey on the men's minds. I reckon we need a man strong enough to scare off any prowlers. How about that black man, Joshua Grant, Jock?"

"He'd fit in real good an' he can be trusted," Miller agreed.

"Is that okay with you women?" Mark asked Dona Estrella.

"It is fine with us."

So it was arranged. They got shovels out of the toolbox under the wagon bed and buried Pablo. Clay Walters rode away to escape the hard labor of digging a grave. When Pablo had been buried without a marker to arouse the curiosity of any chance wayfarer, Mark dismissed Jock Miller.

"You catch up with the herd, Jock. I'll drive the wagon until we reach the bedding grounds tonight. Joshua can take over in the morning."

Mark climbed to the driver's seat of the big wagon and Delma insisted on sitting beside him.

"How do you think this stupid situation is going to resolve itself, Mark? You've got Doby Evers's men on your crew, men that can't be trusted. I've got a hunch that Evers sent Clay Walters and his other men down here not entirely out of mercy for the storm victims, but to see that you don't reach your government lease before the deadline is up. You've got three Mexican *vaqueros* who, free of the sobering influence of Luis Velasco, may be plotting against you. We still don't know if Pablo was poisoned deliberately, or if he died from natural causes. We should have gotten married in Santa Barbara where there was a *padre* to perform the ceremoney even if he was out of his head."

"I've told you before, you're too young to be a widow, sweetheart," Mark admonished her.

"That's better than being an old maid," she retorted.

"That you will never be, Delma. You'll have a man if you have to rope and hogtie him yourself."

"So that's what you think of me—I'm a hussy, is that it?"

"You ain't no shrinkin' violet," Mark told her, "for which I am glad. If things turn out all right, you're goin' to be the mother of our kids. Sometimes a mother has to show her fangs to protect her young, just like a she wolf."

"You'd better stop while you're ahead, Mark Nelson. I'm not a she wolf and I have no fangs. I can be a cuddly kitten, soft and warm, if you'd take the trouble to find out."

"I know what you can be, honey. You can be all things at the proper time. Once we get settled, you can cuddle me to death," he told her.

Due to the long delay, the moon came out before they reached the place where the herd was bedded down. To keep friction to a minimum, Mark had the three Mexican *vaqueros* act as the wranglers of the remuda. The *vaqueros* had a *manana* way of doing things, which irked the American cowboys, so by keeping them separated, things ran more smoothly. Teach had objected to the arrangement.

"Them greasers could run off our remuda during the night. They could sell the horses or trade 'em off," Teach had pointed out.

"Not out here they can't. There ain't no place to sell or trade anything. Mebbe when we get closer to Agua Prieta or the American border they might try something, but by that time I'll make different arrangements," Mark had argued.

By the time he had the wagon parked, Elena, the duenna who did the cooking for the women on the sheet-iron stove in one corner of the wagon, was out of patience with everybody.

"How I am going to cook eef you no stop the wagon?" she demanded of Mark. "We need more wood for the stove. It ees dark now for gather wood. We need also more *agua*."

"Hold it, Elena." Mark held up his hand. "I'll go over to the chuck wagon and see if they have any hot food left over. I'll have Joshua bring over some water. Pablo's death threw us off schedule. Tomorrow we'll get things straightened out."

"I'll go with you, Mark," Delma said. "I can help carry the food."

Mark was about to object but he held his tongue. A roundup camp was no place for a lady. The men, if not forewarned, would be using language and telling ribald jokes unfit for female consumption. Not that Delma was a prude. He was sure she had heard all the words and some of the jokes before. Dale Ford, her father, had sometimes forgotten that she was a girl and had exposed her to rough company as though she were a boy.

On the way over Mark stopped at the remuda and told the Mexican wranglers to take care of the team on the big wagon. He found Joshua Grant helping the cook clear away the remains of the supper. Luckily they had some hot beans with some cubes of side meat in them, and sourdough biscuits still warm in the dutch oven.

"This will do fine, Herby," Delma assured Herb Elder, who had taken over the job of cooking when they left Santa Barbara. Herb worked for Dale Ford and had learned camp cooking from Skillet Kemper, the regular cook on the DF ranch.

"Do you want some canned fruit to go with the beans?" Herb asked.

"We have canned fruit in our wagon, Herby."

Herb had long hair that hung to his shoulders and a wedge-shaped face, but he was usually good-natured, with a toothy grin under his hooked nose.

"You bring some water, Joshua," Mark told the big black man.

"I sure will, Mistah Mark. Mistah Miller done tole me I'm to drive the women's wagon now that Pablo is dead. I aim to keep it stocked up with wood an' whatevah. And I'll see that nothin' happens to the ladies."

"I've got faith in you, Josh," Mark told him. "We'll be headin' through the hills in a day or so, to come out on the Chihuahua Plateau. We could run into trouble."

"I'll see absolutely no harm comes to the ladies, suh."

As they picked up the pot of beans, the biscuits, and the pot of hot coffee that Herb Elder insisted they take along, Clay Walters, with his usual grin, came over from the campfire the drovers had built.

"Can I help you with that stuff?" he inquired, reaching for the pan of biscuits that Delma had already picked up.

"No thank you, Clay. I think we can manage," Delma said, turning her back on him.

Unruffled, Clay turned his attention to Mark. "Don't you think it's a mistake to have the black man look after the women?"

"What do you mean by that, Clay?" Mark asked.

"They won't be able to see him after dark." Walters guffawed over his own remark.

"I advise you not to prowl around our wagon after dark, Clay. You won't be able to see him, but you'll soon learn where he is. You might lose your scalp of wavy blond hair."

"I was just funnin' with you, Delma. Why don't you women come over to the bonfire after you eat? We can sing some songs an' break the monotony," Clay told her. "Us men ain't poison. We can be sweet as sugar plums around proper ladies."

"I'll ask the others," Delma said.

Back at the wagon, the women insisted that Mark share the food with them. Elena was a little miffed and belittled the supper out of hurt pride.

Her complaints didn't stop her from doing justice to her share of the food. Mark marveled at the clever way in which the interior of the wagon was constructed to take advantage of the confined space. Four bunks were hinged on the sidewalls and folded up against the wall when not in use. The sheet-iron stove in the one corner provided heat when needed and a cooking surface. There was a cupboard beside the stove and the table on which they were eating, folded up when it wasn't being used.

"Open a can of fruit, Elena," Dona Estrella suggested.

They discussed the matter of joining the drovers at the bonfire. "It might not be a bad idea," Mark opined. "We've got some rough trail ahead of us. Some of the passes in these hills are very narrow. There's a dozen places ideal for an ambush. I hope we make it without trouble. We've got nearly a dozen men in our cavvy, countin' the Mexicans. We've got arms an' ammo. The Yaqui will think twice before attackin' us. There won't be much time for frivolity later on."

"This may be our last shindig," Delma said. "They call this the *Pista del Muerto*, the trail of death, and we're coming to the worst part of it. If you had married me in Santa Barbara, Mr. Nelson," she went on, giving Mark a haughty glance, "you could protect me day and night."

"Ain't you been ridin' that horse long enough?" Mark said tartly, referring to her remarks about marriage. "If we get through this drive, we'll get married proper and with your pa's blessing."

"You're lucky to be married for love, Delma," Magdalena said. "We Mexican aristocrats have to settle for money and position, neither of which is very romantic."

They finished the fruit and headed for the bonfire. Elena stayed behind to clear away the supper dishes. The moonlight gave the night a silver glow. Lolita clung to Mark's left arm and Delma clung to his right arm.

"You're trespassing, Lolita," Delma warned.

"Me no trespass—he fight for me once. That makes him my godfather," Lolita said.

"There's an age limit on godfathers, Lolita. You're grown up. Let go of my man or you'll need more than a godfather to protect you," Delma quipped.

"So you are jealous for him. That ees good, *amiga*. It shows that you love him."

"I don't know if he loves me," Delma said, pouting. "He could have married me by now if he wanted to."

"Can't you girls think of something else to talk about? I don't want none of this banter goin' on when we reach the fire," Mark admonished them.

The conversation around the fire died down when they reached the circle of men. The men greeted them by rising to their feet and taking off their hats. They fidgeted some and expressed their pleasure in stilted phrases.

"Don't stand on formality for our sake," Dona Estrella told them, smiling. "We're the invaders, so just sit down and be comfortable."

Clay Walters appeared with some blankets and spread them out for the women to sit on.

"Can't have you gals sittin' on the bare earth," he said with his broad grin. "They's a few insects crawlin' about. They hunt at night. They like soft, tender skin to stick their needles in."

"Thanks for the blankets," Delma said, "but no thanks for your scary information. I've made a deal with the scorpions and the tarantulas; I leave them alone and they leave me alone."

They all sat down, a motley group in the center of the vast wilderness. The flickering flame of the fire cast light and shadow on the rugged, flat planes of the men's faces. Their names were mentioned as the conversation swung back and forth. There was Hank Baker whose shaggy roan hair covered his ears and whose half-moon mustache curved over his lip. There was Lewis Santos, half Mexican and half French. He like Hank worked for Doby Evers. He had a sullen face and deep-set dark eyes. There was Van Under, a man with a rugged face that had a neutral expression, and he also worked for Evers.

Foxy Bogen, with his head of kinky curls, and Cappy Steele and Ron Jackson worked for Dale Ford as did Jock Miller. Mark sat next to Delma, feeling the warmth of her near him. Teach and Nagle sat between the other women.

The men told stories of their adventures in the West, careful to eliminate any profanity or vulgarity. They discussed the horrible ordeal of the hurricane and then one of the *vaqueros* who had stayed in the background produced an undersized guitar and he raised his voice in plaintive Mexican song. Soon most of the others joined in the singing. Mark's voice blended with Delma's as he held his arm around her and she lay her head on his shoulder. Mark wondered if this pleasant moment might turn into a nightmare. He studied the men's faces trying to read their minds. It was an impossible task.

Clay Walters was Doby Evers's foreman and Mark felt sure the men under him would obey his instructions in spite of the bribe that he, Mark, had offered them. There was always somebody with a bigger bribe; Doby Evers, for instance. Doby was land hungry, needing all the range he could buy or steal to keep his growing herd of cattle in grass. His herd grew much faster than nature intended. He had been charged with rustling more than once, but never convicted. Two years ago a group of vigilantes got together to stop all rustling on the Culebra Range. There had been a battle between the rustlers and the vigilantes in which four men were killed. Doby wasn't one of the four, and he was never identified with the rustling. Mark thought bitterly that if Doby Evers once got hold of the government lease, nothing but an open fight could dislodge him.

The fire died and the party broke up. At the women's wagon they found Joshua Grant sitting against the wagon wheel beside a pile of mesquite stumps and greasewood branches he had gathered in the moonlight so that Elena would have fuel with which to cook breakfast.

"How's everything, Josh?" Mark greeted him.

"No problems, Mistah Nelson. Ah heard a rattlesnake buzzin' about, but I couldn't find him. Ah reckon the *muchachas* better sleep inside the wagon tonight even if it's crowded."

Delma drew Mark aside. "I don't want to sleep in the wagon, it's too stuffy. I'll put a rope around my bed. The rattlesnakes won't cross it. Why don't you lay your blankets close to mine, honey?"

"Is that what you an' Teach done on your ride down from Douglas?" Mark asked her solemnly.

Her retort was swift and venomous. "Is that what you think of me, Mr. Nelson? Dave Teach is more of a gentleman than you give him credit for!"

"Whoa!" Mark exclaimed. "I'm sorry if I touched a tender spot."

"You'd better quit while you're ahead, *amigo*. What do you mean by a *tender spot*? Teach respected my privacy. Perhaps, in his position, you would have done otherwise," she needled him.

"You know better than that, Del. You offered yourself to me in a marriage by a priest who was befuddled. I refused and gave you my reasons."

"You mean your fear that I might arrive home a widow? At least I would have been your wife a little time."

"But, honey, a widow's life isn't an easy one. She's pitied by some, exploited by others, and distrusted by smugly married wives. She ain't fish, foul, or good red herring. I want something better than that for you."

"It could be the other way around," she reminded him, "you could end up being a widower. If we run into trouble, a bullet is no respecter of age, sex, color, or religion."

"Don't you think that worries me? I aim to protect you with my life if possible. You shouldn't have come down here in the first place. If anything happens to you, your pa'll blame me. It wouldn't make no difference, because without you this whole business would be a grim fiasco."

"Don't blame yourself alone, Mark. We were all to blame. Pa, for putting a price on my marriage. Me, for allowing him to. And you for not telling us both to go to hell."

"Does your pa know you're down here, Del?"

"No. I came on my own. I didn't come down to quarrel with you, honey. I wanted to be near you, to feel you in my arms, to kiss your lips."

Impulsively they kissed good night.

CHAPTER THIRTEEN

They got the herd strung out along the river and headed
for the craggy mountains before the sun was up. Mark
was sharing the point position at the head of the herd
with Clay Walters. Baker and Santos were grudgingly
riding drag, while the others were keeping up the corners.
Most of the wildness had been taken out of the cattle by
the heat of the sun and the rigors of the trail. Mark stared
at the mountains into which they were heading. They were
a jumble of forbidding ledges and peaks through which
the river had carved its way during a million years of
effort. It would take three or four days to reach the high
plateau on which the river found its source.

Mark thought of that warm good-night kiss he had
shared with Delma. It was almost like a final good-bye

embrace. The next few days would be through country infested with Indians, bandits, and bands of Comancheros, led by renegade white men. There were meadows at spots where the herd could be bedded down and find grass to restore their energy. There were also narrow gorges through which the cattle had to be driven three and four abreast. His biggest worry was the wagon load of women that must keep ahead of the herd. It was a prime target for any sniper lurking on the ledges and peaks on either side of the canyon. The sniper might spare the women if he knew of their presence in the wagon, but he would kill the horses pulling the wagon.

At the noon break Mark rode ahead to the wagon. Joshua Grant had unhitched the team to let it graze on the lush grass. The women came out of the wagon to stretch their legs while Elena fixed their lunch.

Mark reached Magdalena first. "How are you women making out?" he inquired.

"The trail's rough, but we manage, Mark."

"Your father was a fool to send you on this trip."

"Mexico is made up of fools, *amigo*. That's why they have so many revolutions. Mexico is ruled not by sense and law, but by bullets and bullies. Maximilian found that out too late. Diaz tries to govern, but sometimes he gets rid of opposition by killing it, and sometimes he succumbs to the flattery of the nabobs left behind when Maximilian was executed. Don't tell this, Mark, but if I ever get to the United States, I'll marry any man who'll keep me there—cowboy, bar swamper, or sheepherder."

"I reckon it won't come to that. You might bag a banker, a politician, or some dude who would love havin' a Spanish aristocrat to show off to his rich friends in Saint Louis or New York."

"In which case I wouldn't gain much." She shrugged. "Phony people are the same everywhere. I want to be a woman with a woman's problems, a man's love, and children to spank and raise."

"There ain't no tellin' how things will turn out, Magdalena. I don't mind tellin' you that we're in a chancy spot. I wish to God that Luis Velasco hadn't got his throat cut. He knew the Indians, he knew these hills, he could keep the three *vaqueros* we still have in line."

"You can do that, Mark."

"I might if I wasn't havin' you women to worry over."

"All I can suggest, Mark, is for you to stop worrying about us. This is isolated country. Perhaps nobody will know we are passing through, unless someone informs them of the fact. We have guns in the wagon, remember? If we have to use them we shall."

Mark reached Delma, who was alone for a moment. She looked at him with a reserved patience. Mark wanted to hold her and repeat the kiss of the night before, but he knew that every such encounter would make their situation harder to bear. He repeated the conversation he had had with Magdalena.

"I talked with Joshua Grant," she told him. "He suggested we women pull away from the herd and travel alone, keeping to the cover of the trees as much as possible. If there are any marauders, the dust and noise of the herd will attract them. If the Indians are after cattle, they'll attack the herd and we'll be a safe distance ahead of it."

Mark considered this. He beckoned to Joshua, who was watching the horses. When Joshua joined them, his face was a solemn mask.

"Josh, Delma tells me you favor getting the women ahead of the herd so they'll be out of danger if there is an attack," Mark said.

"Yes, suh, I 'splained to her how we all might be safer if we ain't connected with the herd. This here trail ain't used much, but it's fairly passable all the way to the top. The cattle will attract any rustlers or adventurous peons. We might reach Douglas ahead of you an' let 'em know you're on the way."

"What do you think of it, Del?" Mark asked.

"It sounds logical to me, Mark, except that I don't want to leave you. I've been on roundups before and I can ride and shoot as well as most men. I'll stay with you and the herd. The wagon is crowded anyhow, and I prefer to sleep on the ground, under the stars."

"I ain't fond of that idea, honey," Mark objected. "If there is a raid it will come at night. Even with the moonlight, it'll be hard to recognize anybody. If bullets start flyin', they ain't gonna be particular who they hit."

"Just look on me as one of the boys like my pa does," she told him. "He won't admit I'm a female until I have a child. I'm going with the herd regardless."

Mark knew the folly of trying to dissuade her. He called the women together and explained the plan Joshua had suggested.

Dona Estrella said, "It's as good a plan as any. Nothing is safe or sacred in this godforsaken country."

Delma caught up her saddle horse which Joshua had

untied from the back of the wagon, and rode with Mark back to the chuck wagon where the men were finishing up their noon meal. He and Delma stopped near Teach and Nagle, who were seated on the ground eating. They rose at the sight of Delma, and Jock Miller came over and joined them. Mark told them of the new plan.

"Them women can complicate things," Miller said, shoving his rusty hair under his Stetson. "We'd be better off if they had stayed behind."

"I told Dona Estrella that, and she lectured me on the matter with Mexican logic. What I gathered was that she felt as safe here as she would in Guadalajara. Accordin' to her any bandit with enough followers could become a Mexican president any time he chose."

"What about you, Delma Ford?" Miller asked. "Your pa'll have my scalp if anything happened to you."

"Pa isn't in the scalp business, Jock," Delma retorted. "This is my affair."

"Ain't nothin' gonna happen to Del," Teach said solemnly. "Me an' Nagle will see to that."

By the time they got the herd on the trail, the wagon had disappeared from the upper end of the meadow. Mark and Delma rode swing for the rest of the day. It was an easy position. With the river on one side and the canyon wall on the other, the cattle could not stray far. Secretly Mark was glad to have Delma with him though he soft-pedaled any romantic demonstration. It made him feel good just to have her near him, and he marveled at how expertly she kept the cattle in line. She was a Western girl inured to the demands of the wild country. Her father's obsession for having a boy, which he was denied, had saddled her with the task of fulfilling his wish by being his companion not only at home, but on the range and during roundup time. In spite of her dexterity with gun and spur, she was still a woman with a woman's dreams. He hoped to fulfill her dreams when he got his ranch established.

The second day after the women's wagon had pulled ahead of the drive, Mark awoke to find the Mexican *vaqueros* gone. He went to the remuda expecting to find the horses gone with them, but the horses were still there. Teach came over to the rope corral.

"Where's the hoss wranglers, Mark?" Teach asked.

"Damned if I know. They usually have the cayuses watered by this time," Mark said. "They can't be far off or they would have taken the horses with them. They didn't stop for their pay or nothin'. This is a spot where Luis Velasco would come in handy."

Jock Miller came over. "What happened to the Mexicans?" he inquired.

"I reckon they snuck off during the night, but I can't see them going emptyhanded," Teach said.

"Mebbe they figure to fill their hand some other way," Mark mused.

Miller shook his head. "I don't savvy this. They didn't look smart enough to come in out of the rain. If they walked off without the horses, they'll be back."

"Yeah," Mark added, "but they may not be alone. They've got more savvy about this wild country and the Indians than anybody in our cavvy. They're half Indian themselves. Pick out a couple of men to wrangle the horses, Jock. All we can do is move on an' keep our eyes an' ears open."

"What can three peons do against us, Mark? Unless—unless..." Delma's voice trailed off.

"Unless what, honey?" Mark prompted her.

"Unless they know of Yaquis close by whom they could join up with," she said.

"Keep your hair under your hat, an' pretend to be a man, Delma   case they do come around."

They moved the herd up the steep trail, through gorges so narrow part of the herd had to wade in the river. Toward evening they reached a wide spot on the trail with plenty of grass for the cattle to feed on. Although there was still an hour or two of daylight, Mark decided to bed down for the night. It could be a long while before they found another spot suitable. While they were bunching the herd, Mark rode up canyon to the head of the herd to turn the leaders back to the main body. His eyes caught something half hidden in the trees at the side of the clearing. Nudging his horse that way, he was perplexed and disturbed to see the women's wagon standing there. Thinking they might have wrecked a wheel or broken an axle on the rough trail, he approached the wagon.

"Hyah, there! What's wrong, Josh?" he called out as he neared the wagon.

He was greeted by silence. A strange fear crept up his spine, and he fought back an overwhelming desire to rush the wagon with a drawn gun. The women could be out in the trees stretching their legs. His fear wouldn't subside though. Josh should have stayed with the wagon. He had expected the wagon to be farther ahead by now, but the trail had been rough and it could have held them back. Then he noticed that the horses were gone.

"What's goin' on here, Josh?" he shouted.

There was still no answer. Teach and Delma rode up behind him.

"What's all the shoutin' about, Mark?" Teach inquired.

"There's something wrong here, Red," Mark said, urgency in his voice. "The wagon should have been farther ahead of us."

They reached the wagon without further comment, their silence more potent than words. Mark rode close to the door of the wagon and jerked it open. The interior had been ransacked. There was no sign of the women!

"Good Lord," Delma half-whispered, "the women have been kidnapped!"

Mark leaned over and squeezed her arm. "Thank God, you insisted on staying with the herd, honey." The enormity of what the empty wagon implied forced an oath from his lips.

Teach had dismounted and climbed into the wagon. Mark joined him. They looked for clues as to what kind of devils had perpetrated the crime.

"What do you think, Mark?" Teach asked.

"I think that whoever named this trail the *Pista del Muerto* knew what they were talkin' about. Do you realize what might happen to the women?" Mark asked.

"If they was captured by the Indians they might have a slim chance to be held for ransom. But they's others worse than the Indians—the Comancheros. The Comancheros would relish havin' an' aristocrat to fondle. Then they'd ask for a ransom," Teach said solemnly.

"I know—I know." Mark nodded. "It was my fault for lettin' them go ahead of the herd."

"Don't play the martyr just yet, my love," Delma cautioned him. "It was Joshua's idea that the women travel ahead of the herd. There could be a connection here between the missing *vaqueros* and the attack on the women. The *vaqueros* disappeared during the night. They knew the women had left the herd. They could have induced the attackers to capture the women and hold them for ransom."

"Standin' here talkin' ain't goin' to do no good," Mark said, tight-lipped. "We gotta go back to the herd an' form a search party before it gets dark."

"It's close to dark now," Teach said. "We can't start a ruckus until we're sure the women are safe."

"Safe?" Mark spat the word. "They ain't goin' to be safe while they're in the hands of devils!"

"Have you got a notion they'll be safer with bullets in 'em?" Teach said.

"We can't go off half-cocked," Delma warned them. "We've got to know where they are, how they're being held, and what their captors want. The situation calls for caution."

"Let's get back to the herd and report what's happened," Mark said. His heart was like lead, and his mind a knot of conflicting ideas. His impulse was to track the fiends who had captured the women, and kill them without mercy, but he knew how futile that would be. As long as the women were in jeopardy, they had to proceed cautiously, as Delma had pointed out.

The herd was between them and the camp at the site of the chuck wagon. They rode around the herd on the hill side and when they reached the camp they were confronted by a scene that astounded them! It was beyond all reason and reality. The men stood near the chuck wagon their hands at their sides. Across the river that had narrowed in the canyon stood a row of nondescript bandits with rifles at the ready. The three *vaqueros* were among them. The leader, a heavy man with tassels on his sombrero and bandoleers full of ammunition crisscrossed from his shoulders, was shouting words in broken English. Jock Miller and Clay Walters were facing the man keeping their hands away from their guns. Mark took in the situation at a glance. Death hung over the river, ready to strike should one gun be fired.

"What's going on here?" Mark demanded as he reached Miller's side.

"We've been ambushed. These greasers threaten to wipe us out unless we give them everything—guns, cattle, and horses," Miller explained.

"They've already got the women. Their wagon is up the trail in the trees. It's been ransacked. There ain't no sign of them or Joshua Grant." Mark turned his attention to the bandit leader across the narrow stretch of water. "What have you done with the women?" he demanded.

"Me no savvy," the leader said.

"You savvy, all right. If you harm those women you'll all be killed!"

"No, senor, it ees you who will be killed," the big man said, preening his drooping moustache. He turned and said something in Spanish to the men with the cocked rifles. They nodded. Some of them grinned.

Mark realized the danger in the situation. Keeping his voice steady, he said, "What do you want to turn the women loose unharmed?"

"The *muchachas* and the *senoras* are much beautiful." The man smirked.

"How much?" Mark repeated.

"Your guns, senor. Your cattle."

"You go plumb to hell!" Clay Walters shouted.

"After you, senor!" the leader shouted back, and fired point blank.

Walters was spun around, drawing his gun as he fell, his hip wounded. He fired a wild shot. The rifles across the stream spat flame. There was no need to go to hell. Hell had come to them!

"Get down!" Mark shouted to the drovers, falling to his stomach and slithering behind the chuck wagon.

Guns roared from both sides of the stream. The bandits charged through the shallow water, pumping their rifles as they came. Mark, tried to get a bead on the leader of the bandits, but the confusion blocked his view. With a pang he remembered Delma. She was in the midst of the slaughter. He had to find her, protect her. He yelled her name but his voice was swallowed up by the guns, the shouts, and the cries of the dying as lead smashed into them. His gun jumped in his hand—once, twice! Two of the bandits fell, screaming for the protection of the God they had defied. The drovers fired from a prone position matching their side arms against the rifles of the bandits. It was difficult in the cloud of dust and the waning light to tell friend from foe. Mark rolled from under the wagon. A bandit raised his gun to smash the butt into the head of a man he straddled. Mark launched himself, hit the bandit in the small of his back, and sent him sprawling. A shot in the head finished the man off. Mark turned to where the man's intended victim lay. He heard a whimpering voice calling his name.

"Mark—Mark, where are you?"

It was Delma's voice. He crawled back to protect her with his body. He had no time to answer her. He fired carefully so as not to shoot one of his own men. There were ominous sounds from the herd of cattle. There was bawling, the stamping of hooves, the raucous bellows of terror. If the herd stampeded downstream, they would trample them all. Mark carefully dragged Delma's limp body under the chuck wagon.

"Mark, is that you?"

"I'm here, honey."

"I've been hit, Mark. Don—don't leave me."

"I'll never leave you, darling."

He had three shots left. He could fire at the herd to stop it, or he could fire at the bandits to kill them. Through a break in the dust he saw the bandit leader slashing about himself with a bolo knife. The cattle were coming at the bandit who tried to reach the river. Mark took careful aim. He dropped the bandit leader with a shot to his head. The big man feel under the hooves of the terrified beasts! The herd split around the wagon. Some of them tripped over the tongue and were trampled by those who stumbled over them. The shooting died down, and the bawling of the terrified beasts, and the drumming of their hooves passed them. In the dim light as the dust settled,

Mark saw the big figure of Joshua Grant waving a smoking gun and mouthing a voodoo chant! He looked at the black man with wonder. Where were the women? There was no time to ask the question. Delma stirred.

"Mark—Mark," she whimpered. "I—I'm hurt, Mark."

"Lay still, darling. I'll get a blanket to cover you with." Mark wondered how many had died, how many drovers, how many bandits? The fight had been short but deadly.

Herb Elder, who had taken over the cook's job, came from the inside of the chuck wagon. He had a lantern in his hand. He held it close to Mark and Delma.

"My heavens, what a ruckus! I lay on the floor under my bunk till the hell simmered down. Is that a girl you're coddlin'?"

"My girl, Herb. I need a blanket."

"The inside of the chuck wagon is still in good shape. Bring her in onto my bunk. I guarantee there ain't no lice or bedbugs in it," Herb said.

Joshua Grant came to the circle of light. Mark didn't ask him about the women; that could wait. "Give me a hand with her, Josh," Mark said.

They gently took her inside the wagon and placed her on the narrow bunk. It was a miracle that the chuck wagon was still intact.

"Go out, Josh, and look things over. We gotta take care of the wounded. The dead can wait," Mark told him.

CHAPTER FOURTEEN

With the lantern hanging over the bunk, Mark looked down at Delma and felt a surge of pity. A stab of fear wracked him. Her eyes were open, staring at him, and there was a glassy shine to them. For a moment he thought she might be dead. A movement of her lips denied his fear and he realized the glassiness was caused by unshed tears.

"Am I bleeding much, Mark?" she whispered.

Mark wished fervently that one of the women were there to tend her. "I'll have to open your shirt, honey, to find the wound."

"It—it's in my side, Mark," she told him.

With fumbling fingers he found the wound. It was more painful than dangerous. Herb Elder had gone outside the chuck wagon because of the restricted space. Now Mark called to Herb.

"Have you got any whiskey or tequila, Herb?"

"There's a bottle I keep for medicinal purposes in the cupboard at the head of the bunk. It's far back o' the canned beans kinda hid. Mebbe I'd better get it fur ya."

"I'll find it, Herb. I could use come hot water."

"My woodpile is scattered from hell to breakfast, Mark. The water in the barrel is still warm from the heat o' the sun."

"That will have to do. Are there any clean rags or dishtowels in here?"

"They's some hangin' over the pothooks. They ain't snowy white. Give me a pot an' I'll hand you some water."

"Make it fast, Herb."

Delma made no sound during the exchange of words. While Mark searched out the bottle of whiskey, she said, "Is—is it real bad, Mark?"

"No, it ain't," Mark assured her, "but I reckon it's surely sore an' painful. I'm goin' to wash the blood away. It's a shallow wound. The bullet went in your side and came out the back after skidding off your ribs."

Herb handed the pot of water through the slit in the canvas that served as a door. Mark washed the coagulating blood away. He turned her over enough to reach the ragged hole where the bullet had emerged.

"I'm goin' to cauterize the wound with whiskey, honey, so grit your teeth," he warned her.

She stiffened as the whiskey burned into the wound, but she made no outcry. Mark took one of the not-so-white dishtowels, tore it into strips. He was about to try and lift her shoulders so that he could bind the strips around her when she grabbed his arm and pulled herself to a sitting position.

"I'm not helpless now that I know the wound is superficial," she said. "It scared the hell out of me, though. I've never been shot before."

"You never will again if I have anything to say about it," Mark vowed. "The *trail of death* is living up to its name. I came down here hoping to buy cheap cattle. They're turning out to be damned expensive."

"It was the hurricane that defeated you, honey. If Luis Velasco had not been murdered, he could have handled the *vaqueros* and even the Yaquis. There probably won't be another storm like that for twenty or thirty years," she reassured him as he finished bandaging her.

By the time Mark got outside, Herb had a fire going. Joshua came back, with Teach and Miller. Joshua held a resinous torch in his hand which he had hacked off a tree.

"What did you men find?" Mark inquired, dreading their answer.

"I ain't never seen so much blood an' death in such a short time in my born days," Teach said. "Santos an' Cappy Steele are dead. Clay Walters is layin' up yonder. He got a bullet through his hip. Hank Baker is with him. He bandaged Clay's wound."

"Did you see Rex Nagle anywhere?" Mark asked.

"Never seen no sign of him," Teach said.

"Did you see him anywhere, Josh?" Mark asked the black man.

"No, suh. Ah seen dead men, mostly bandits. Ah reckon two of the bandits got away. Ah seed them scrabblin' through the trees and bushes. Mebbe Mistah Nagle has gone after 'em," Joshua hazarded.

"Where did they hide the women, Josh?"

"Ah hain't got no recollect 'bout that, suh. Ah seen them *bandidos* when they was down rivah. I drove the wagon up yondah into the trees, turned the hosses loose an' told the women to hide out back away from the rivah. I messed up the wagon to look like it had already been ransacked. Then I hid out, hopin' to protect the women, but the bandits never reached the wagon. They fixed to ambush you all right heah, Ah reckon. Ah heard the shootin' down here an' come to he'p you all."

"You did right, Josh," Mark said, "but if two bandits escaped, they might run into the women an' take their spite out on them. We can't track 'em in the dark. At first crack of light we'll have to clean up this mess, look for the women an' gather up the cattle."

Mark went back into the chuck wagon to be near Delma. She was asleep or unconscious, he didn't know which, but he didn't try to wake her. The day had been hell for all of them. He couldn't think of a worse tragedy. He canceled that thought. The women were still unaccounted for. He lay down in the narrow space beside Delma's bunk, and tried to sleep.

In the gray dawn Herb had coffee steaming and fatback and beans cooking on the camp stove which had escaped destruction. The men gathered around, still half asleep. There was still no sign of Rex Nagle. If he was pursuing the two bandits who had escaped he should have caught up with them by now. Horrible as the attack had been, it could have been worse. The bandits had no doubt expected to mow them all down in the first fusillade. Only the uncertain light, the bad marksmanship of the killers, and the swift response of the drovers had saved them from complete annihilation.

Before eating, Mark went down to the river to slosh water on his face. There he was dealt another blow. He thought he was immune to shock, but the sight of Rex Nagle's body bobbing gently in the backwash of the water on the river's bank stunned him like a shaft of pain. Nagle had been a killer, an outlaw banished from his native country, but he was also a man—a man on whom friendship and loyalty had struck a lethal blow. Mark felt the hot sting of tears, and marveled that he had come through the horrible fight dry-eyed, and was now weeping over a man who had already been condemned to death by the laws of civilized men. Perhaps this final sacrifice might expunge some of the black marks on Rex Nagle's record.

Mark went back to the chuck wagon and told them about Nagle. They accepted the grim news in stony silence. He gave orders to Jock Miller to have the men drag the bodies of the bandits into the gulch beside the road and cover them with rocks.

"I reckon that Nagle, Santos, and Cappy Steele deserve better than that. Dig them a grave but leave no marker. Me an' Josh is goin' after the women. After the burials, bunch the herd. I'm not goin' to lose the herd after all the blood that has been spent on them."

He went in to see how Delma was and found her awake and sitting up on the bunk. He didn't tell her about Rex Nagle. There would be time for that later.

"You're supposed to be layin' down, Del. That bullet could have struck your heart. Herb Elder will get you what you need."

"I need you, Mark. I had no idea that we'd have to go through hell to claim each other," she said.

He told her about the women and how they were hiding out in the chaparral. He didn't mention the two bandits who had escaped. It would only upset her. He kissed her tenderly and recalled her words that he might arrive in Douglas a widower. Those words had almost proved prophetic. He left her determined to live and see that she lived. Finding Joshua Grant, he asked him to come along to search for the women.

"You know approximately where they might be found, Josh," he explained.

"Fact is, Mistah Nelson, Ah ain't no readah of a female's mind, but females know how to hide themselves. I'm obliged you asked me along, suh. I was about to go lookin' for them myself. A'm responsible for them, I reckon."

"We're all responsible for them, Josh. Here, take this gun an' gunbelt. It belonged to one of the bandits. Be careful what you shoot at. We don't want to harm the women."

They went up to the end of the clearing where the wagon was hidden in the trees. Nothing had been further disturbed in the wagon. The trail left by the horses could be easily followed, but trailing the women was a difficult matter. They had covered their tracks very well. Mark turned to Joshua.

"You take that first gulch that leads away from the

river, I'll take the other one farther upstream."

"Iffen I find them, suh, you want I should fire my gun to signal you?"

"No, Josh. There's still two bandits on the loose. A gunshot would only warn them of our presence. Just take whoever you find back to the camp," Mark told him.

"I reckon you're right, Mistah Nelson."

"Just call me Mark, like everybody else, Josh."

"Force of habit, suh. Ah was borned a slave in Virginny. Ah got 'mancipated young, but I never forgot the old ways, suh."

Just then they heard a gunshot inside the gulch they were facing. "Get down, Josh! Reckon them convicts has spotted us!" Mark warned, rolling from the saddle.

Instead of dismounting, Josh rode pell-mell up the gulch. The women were his responsibility and he meant to protect them at the risk of his own life. Mark chose a more cautious approach. He made his way swiftly through the chaparral and bushes, determined to back up Josh's play. He broke into a clearing and there he saw all four of the women at the mouth of a small cave. Lolita Sanchez had a gun in her hand. Mark breathed a prayer of thanks at finding them unharmed. He made his way to them as fast as he could.

"Thank God you're safe!" Mark exclaimed when he reached them.

"Thank Lolita," Magdalena said. "Two of the horrible men were coming up the gully, but she scared them off with the gun."

"You mean the men were just here?" Mark queried.

"No, *amigo*," Lolita said, "eet was last night. Still some

shots were being fired down below. I shoot just in case you were looking for us. I take this gun from the wagon for our protection."

"You're a brave *muchacha*, Lolita. Let's get out of here an' back to the wagon. You women must be starved."

"Ah reckon ah'll find the hosses an' git the wagon back in shape, suh," Josh said. "The women's saddle hosses is runnin' loose with the team. By the time you all git the cattle rounded up, the wagon will be ready to roll."

Back at the camp the women sat down to a welcome meal. The drovers were out looking for the herd, except for the three who were finishing the burial of the bandits in the gully and covering them with rocks. Mark saw the mounds of earth along the river bank where the drovers were buried in shallow graves with no markers to disclose their final resting place to greedy men eager for spoil.

Mark went to where Clay Walters sat, favoring his leg. "How's your wound, Clay?"

"I'll live. I reckon there ain't any gangrene set in yet."

"Were any of the Mex *vaqueros* who were working with us among the dead?" Mark asked.

"Only one of 'em, Mark. The other two must have skeedaddled."

"They could give us trouble later on," Mark opined.

He hurried to the bunk in the chuck wagon and with a worried frown found Delma lying quietly, her eyes closed. Her face was flushed and when he put his hand on her forehead, it confirmed the fact that she had a fever. He didn't know if she was asleep or unconscious. Her lips moved but she didn't open her eyes.

"Is that you, Mark?" she asked weakly.

"It's me, honey."

"I hurt, Mark. I feel hot all over."

"I think your wound needs lookin' at, Del. Gangrene must be settin' in. I'll get one of the women to come change the bandage."

Mark went to where the women were finishing their breakfast. He explained to Dona Estrella about Delma's wound. "It needs draining and a clean bandage. I poured booze on the jagged wound, but I didn't pour enough or the booze was no good."

"I'll take care of her, Mark," Lolita said. "My *madre*, she has theengs for bullet wounds. I weel find, here in this place of death, the theengs that also geeve life. It will pay you back for the fight for me."

Sick at heart for the evil that dogged him, Mark went out to help gather the scattered cattle.

Two days later the herd was bunched with only a few head lost to the stampede. Lolita had made a poultice of herbs which she applied to Delma's wound after cauterizing the infection, and Delma was doing well. Herb Elder insisted that she remain in his bunk at least until they reached the plateau. Josh had recovered the horses and put the big wagon in proper order.

Mark, who was riding swing with Teach, said, "It looks like we're through with bad luck. We'll be on the plateau in another day and there'll be no place for an ambush there."

"Keep your fingers crossed, Mark. Those two Mex drovers who escaped during the fight are still on the loose."

"They can't rustle the herd by theirselves," Mark said.

"They can stir up some other mischief at the border. And don't forget Evers. He may already have his cattle on your range. It might be a fight if you try to drive him off."

"Everything's a fight here in the West, Teach. The man who won't fight for what's his, ends up as a swamper, a bullcook, or a drunk. The way I figure I've still got ten days time to get my cattle on that lease. Besides I get ten days grace more if I run into trouble. I sure as hell ran into trouble."

"Amen," Teach said piously. "You might run into more trouble afore this ruckus is over. Evers has a tough crew. Some of 'em are still here in the cavvy. Who knows what Clay Walters will do in a showdown?"

"We'll cross that bridge when we come to it, Teach. We've still got a few men of our own. The wagons that brought the relief supplies to Santa Barbara should have reached the border long before now. Who knows what's goin' on in Douglas? I've got friends across the border," Mark reminded him.

They reached the plateau and the ordeal of the drive up the tortuous canyon was over. Unexpected rain had revived the graze and adequate food took the last dregs of wildness out of the cattle. Delma's wound had healed nicely and she rode with Mark part of the day and insisted on sleeping on the ground near him during the night. The women's wagon, on Mark's orders, had pulled ahead of the herd and was now out of sight. It should reach Douglas days before the herd arrived at the border. Mark had planned it that way because if there was a confrontation at the border and a fight broke out, the women would not only be in danger, they would be in the way.

During a hot afternoon, Delma, riding beside Mark at point, said, "You're going to make it Mark, even with the horrible troubles you've had you're going to make it."

"What'll your pa think about it? I ain't sure he'll be pleased. You're all he has to live for, sweetheart. The thought that another man is going to steal you away from him won't be exactly joyful."

"He'll get over it if we give him a grandson," she said smugly.

"Another day we'll be near the border. I want you, Del, to ride ahead. Go see your pa an' tell him we're comin'. Evers might try to stop us, or delay us until the deadline on my lease runs out. He could claim we had hoof and mouth disease in the herd an' that could hold us up for days waitin' for an inspector to come down from Phoenix or Tucson. He might try to attack us south of the border where the U.S. marshal has no jurisdiction. I can't have you caught in another fight, honey. If there's anything buildin' up there to keep me from crossin' the border, send a man back with the news. Don't you come yourself."

CHAPTER FIFTEEN

The following day Delma took off at dawn for the border that was some eight miles north. Mark called the men together. He separated Evers's men from Ford's men. He spoke first to Evers's men.

"I promised you men," he told them, "I'd pay you a bonus if and when I got this herd across the border. Your boss, Evers, ain't goin' to welcome me with open arms. If it comes to a fight, I ain't sure which side you'd be on. I reckon it would be on Evers's side, loyal to your own ranch. I ain't blamin' you for that, so I'm payin' you off now with bank drafts that'll include your bonus. I'll have my hands full without havin' to make sure you ain't about to shoot me in the back."

Clay Walters, who had regained the use of his leg,

spoke up. "What makes you think we'll go easy with you in a fight because we got your bank drafts in our pocket? After all, the bank drafts might not be any good."

"They're good, Walters."

"How about the men who were killed in the fight with the bandits?" Walters asked. "They ain't goin' to be cashin' no bank drafts, good or bad."

"Rex Nagle was a condemned man before the fight. If Santos and Cappy Steele have any kin, I'll settle with them," Mark said grimly.

So it was arranged. Van Under, running his fingers through his hair, said, "I'll take my pay, but I ain't goin' back to Evers. He's broke eleven of the good Lord's commandments. He rustled, robbed, and murdered to get where he is. When I sell my soul it will be to a righteous man."

"Wait a minute, Under," Clay Walters said. "You ain't been so particular up to now. Why the sudden change of heart?"

"I ain't gonna fight against Mark Nelson. He's gone through hell to get this bunch of dogies this far. He's earned the right to put this herd on his range, an' I ain't gonna kill or get killed to stop him."

"In that case you'd better not show your face in Douglas," Walters said, dropping all pretenses. "You know what Evers told us when we came south with the rations for the peons. He wasn't sendin' them supplies out of the goodness of his heart. He sent them so we could cozy up to Mark Nelson and stop this herd from reaching the border. Well, our scheme failed back yonder, but there's still time to stop it."

"You mean that you arranged the ambush in the mountains?" Mark said, his eyes narrowing.

"I reckon I planned it different, but you can't trust a Mex. I made a deal with the three *vaqueros* who disappeared from the cavvy comin' up the canyon. They was to get some Yaquis to scatter the cows from hell to breakfast. Instead they brought a bunch of Comancheros who decided to kill us and keep the herd an' all our equipment after executin' the lot of us," Walters said calmly.

"You're a dog, Walters!" Mark spat out. "Nagle, Santos, and Steele are dead because of you."

"But I didn't kill them. The bandits did. Too bad *you* didn't get killed in the fight, Nelson. It would have saved a lot of trouble."

Mark's emotions were seething. "My girl nearly got killed, you coyote!"

"She had no business bein' there. She should wear dresses and frilly things like other women, an' stay at home where she belongs. Mebbe there's still time to straighten things out."

"What do you mean by that, Clay?"

"We're still in Mexico. Murder ain't no crime here. It's a pastime. No U.S. marshal has jurisdiction this side of the border," Clay Walters said in a flat, deadly voice, backing away.

Mark stiffened. There was a taut menace in the air. Walters was bracing for a showdown. His sore hip was no handicap. It was on his left side, away from his gun. Mark kept his hands free. He knew where his gun was, and he knew it was loaded. The Ford men backed to one side, and the Evers crew backed to the other side. Mark wanted desperately to stop the shootout here in sight of the border.

"Walters, you're a mite loco. What good would it do to kill me—*if* you do kill me?" Mark asked evenly.

"I'd be rid of you, that's what! I didn't expect you to get this far. With you dead, I can face Doby Evers with a clear conscience."

"I don't kill cripples," Mark said, referring to Clay's hip.

"*You're* not a cripple, Nelson. I got no scruples to stop me!"

Van saw the twitch of Walters's shoulder. Walters's gun was almost clear of his holster when Mark made his draw. He felt the hot breath of Walters's bullet graze his head as he drew and fired in one motion. Walters fell to his knees, his second shot going wild.

"For heaven's sake, stop it, Walters!" Mark cried.

Walters couldn't or wouldn't hear him. He steadied his gun on his elbow, his finger tightening on the trigger. At the same moment a shot rang out from Evers's men. Walters jerked and fell dead. Van Under stood away from Evers's group, a smoking gun in his hand. The other Evers men mounted their horses and rode toward the border, hell for leather.

"God what a mess," Mark lamented, "and right in sight of the border, too. Walters must've gone off his rocker." He turned to Under. "I don't know whether to thank you or cuss you, Van."

"If you was dead you couldn't cuss me or you couldn't thank me," Under said laconically. "Just let it lay like it is. You held your fire, an' I killed a grinning jackass who wasn't no good to the world. I reckon I'll take his advice and steer clear of Douglas," Under said, mounting his horse.

"My draft will be honored in Bixby or Tombstone!" Mark called after him.

"If he hadn't of killed Walters, I would have," Teach said.

Mark said to his other men, Jock Miller, Herb Elder, and Foxy Bogen, "I brought these dogies through fire and brimstone to here. I don't aim to lose them now. How I'm goin' to get 'em across the border I ain't sure. I don't even know how many men Evers has at the border. I don't want no more killing."

"Killin' is no man's pleasure, but there ain't no way to stop it once it starts," Teach said.

"If you men want to get out of this, I'll pay you off here with bank drafts. I hired your guns, sure enough, you understood that. But I thought there'd be more of us for this showdown. I might have to go into Douglas and try to make a deal."

"Hold on there, Mark," Foxy Bogen said, a cigarette dangling from his lips, "we ain't no yellow livers. I ain't never run out on a job because it was dangerous. I ain't goin' to start now."

Herb Elder and Jock Miller repeated his sentiments.

A cloud of dust appeared coming from the direction of the border. As the rider came close, Mark recognized Joshua Grant. Joshua dismounted in front of them.

Mark greeted him warmly. "When did you get to Douglas, Josh?" he queried.

"Four days ago. The women is fine. You cain't beat that bunch for stamina and savvy."

"Did you run into Delma in Douglas?" Mark asked.

"Sure did. Reckon she went out to her father's ranch. She tole me to ride out an' tell you how things was."

"How are they, Josh?"

"Evers hisself is in town. He's got some inspectors—leastways they say they is inspectors—who aim to examine your herd at the border. If he finds any diseased crittahs, he'll order the whole herd kilt off," Josh said.

"I expected something like that. He won't get away with it," Mark vowed.

"He's got a posse of his men to back him up," Josh warned.

"Josh, do you know where the El Lucido silver mine is?"

"Sure do. It ain't far from here."

"You go there and see Alfredo, the superintendent. He's a friend of mine. No, wait, you stay here and help hold the herd until I get back. I'll go to the mine myself. Alfredo will listen to me," Mark explained. "We need some dynamite."

"What you goin' to do with dynamite, boss?" Herb Elder inquired.

"I'll let you know when I get the dynamite," Mark said, mounting his horse.

He had no trouble talking Alfredo out of a dozen sticks of dynamite, a roll of fuse, and a box of detonators. It was after sundown when he got back to the herd. His men were camped on the Douglas side of the herd waiting for any attack from town, but none came. Mark explained his plan.

"We'll ease the herd closer to the border at first light in the morning. We'll cut these sticks of dynamite in half an' put a detonator an' a short fuse with a detonator in each stick. When we get near the border, we'll light the fuses an' toss them in back of an' on the sides of the herd. They'll make a hell of a noise, but they ain't too dangerous. It'll stampede the cattle worse than thunder an' lightnin'. They'll hit the border like an avalanche, an' tromp down anything in their way. Once they're across the border Evers can't do nothin' about them."

"He can start shootin'," Bogen said, "an' he won't waste bullets on the cattle. He'll try to get you first, Mark, an' the rest of us in order."

"We'll shoot back," Mark said quietly. "If he wants a fight we'll oblige him."

At dawn they moved the three thousand head of stock toward the border. Up ahead in the brightening light they saw Evers's armed men awaiting their arrival. Evers, on his big stallion, was in the middle of the line. At a spot near the border, Mark gave the signal. They lit the fuses and tossed the dynamite around the herd. As the deafening explosions split the air, the cattle lunged forward like a juggernaut! The screams of the terrified beasts and the drumbeats of their hooves created a pandemonium of sound and a blinding shroud of dust. Mark and his men rode on their heels, firing their guns. The wall of cattle poured across the border trampling anything that got in their way!

Once across the border, Mark braced himself for a real

battle. In the swirling cloud of dust it was difficult to pick friend from foe. He saw a man pointing a gun at him, and he shot the man out of the saddle. He kept riding forward to get as far inside the border as he could. In one rift in the dust-cloud, he saw Evers livid with rage, yelling at his men to let the cattle go and kill the drovers.

"I want Mark Nelson's hide! This is the last trick he'll pull on me!" Evers screamed.

Mark found himself in a cul-de-sac surrounded by Evers's gunnies. Here at the last moment they were caught in a trap. Mark had hoped to follow the cattle through the town and into the open. He glimpsed Evers again.

"If you want my hide, come and get it!" Mark yelled above the pandemonium.

Evers caught sight of him and turned, firing his gun. The bullet hit Mark in the chest. He didn't feel the pain, only the shuddering blow as the bullet entered his body. He had counted his shots. He had two bullets left in his gun. A haze was forming over his eyes. He heard shots coming from another direction. So this was to be the end of his folly. Evers, dimly visible through the dust, epitomized the cause of his failure. He gripped his gun with both hands. Two shots. They had to count. They had to banish the range hog from the earth. His first shot blasted Evers from his saddle; the second shot hit him in the head as he was trying to rise to his knees. Mark felt the fiery pain in his chest as he sank into a black, peaceful hole of oblivion.

When Mark came to, his vision was fuzzy and he thought he was dreaming. He recognized the interior of the Ford parlor with its hand-hewn ceiling beams and bright Indian tapestries. There were people standing around; Dona Estrella with her mane of dark hair, Magdalena, and her duenna. Then Mark noticed Teach, with his arm in a sling and Lolita fussing over him. Foxy Bogen sat on the floor, a bandage around his head. Finally, as Mark's vision cleared, he recognized someone closer. And with a catch in his throat, he realized that the soft face with the brown eyes belonged to Delma Ford, who was hovering over him.

"Is—is that really you, sweetheart?" he murmured.

She kissed him long and hard on the lips. "Thank God, you came to, Mark. If you had died . . ." Her voice broke in a sob.

"What happened, honey?"

"That stampede that you sent across the border was a foolhardy thing, but it paid off. Evers's phony inspectors who hoped to keep you from crossing got some bones broken for their trouble. Evers was killed I don't know by whom. Two of his men were killed. The rest hightailed it when Pa and his men joined the fight."

"Your pa joined the fight to help *me*?"

Dale Ford came out of the shadows. His clean-cut face was solemn. "I'm sorry I put my daughter on the auction block, Mark. I thought the conditions I had set were beyond your reach, but you proved me wrong. I changed my mind about you when Teach came here alone to beg for relief supplies for the poor people of Santa Barbara. Delma went back with him against my wishes, but her loyalty to you proved that you two belonged together. Them cows you brought with you ain't the fanciest in the world, but we'll fatten them up an' breed them to good bulls."

"What do you mean by *we*, Mr. Ford?" Mark asked puzzled.

"I mean we'll throw our two ranches together. Now that Evers is dead, I can buy his place out. He's heavily in debt to the bank. My place will go to Delma eventually anyway. I want my grandsons born close to home."

Mark looked around as he tried to grasp the situation. "I'm sure glad you made it, Magdalena. I didn't expect to find you here. I thought you'd be on your way to the mission or stayin' at the hotel," he said to her.

"Joshua Grant brought us here. He said that the hotel wasn't fit for us. Mr. Ford generously took us in and insisted we remain here for a while and rest up," she explained.

"Where's Josh? He's a good man, Mr. Ford," Mark said.

"*Was* a good man, Mark," Dale Ford said solemnly. "He was killed in the shootout, trying to protect you after you were shot. And stop callin' me *Mr. Ford*. Pop'll do."

Mark let this sink in. "I reckon he was a better man than me," he said brokenly.

"You can make it up to him, Mark, when we're married. We'll name our first son after him," Delma promised, smothering him with kisses before he could protest.

Mark suddenly found himself with nothing to protest about.